STRANDED IN THE SNOW

HOLIDAY ACRES

NOELLE ADAMS

This book is a work of fiction. Names, characters, places, and incidents are the product of the author's imagination or are used fictitiously. Any resemblance to actual events, locales, or persons, living or dead, is coincidental.

1

Olivia Holiday should have been having a good day. It was just a week until Christmas, it had started snowing an hour ago, and she was helping with the final preparations for a gorgeous wedding at Holiday Acres. But Scott Matheson had just walked through the door with his smug swagger and a pair of jeans that fit his lean body far too well.

Her festive mood took a dramatic nosedive.

She disliked Scott more than anyone else in the world, and that included two asshole ex-boyfriends and Patty Harrison, her high school nemesis, who was still waging a teenage war of aggression against her.

Scott was different.

Scott was worse.

“Why didn’t anyone warn me that the asshole was stopping by?” she asked through her teeth, turning her back to Scott as she spoke.

Laura, the oldest of the four Holiday sisters, was thirty-one and handled the business end of Holiday Acres, the family's sprawling Christmas store and tree farm located in a small town outside Charlottesville, Virginia. She was no-nonsense, slim, and pretty with her brown eyes and freckles. She glanced over Olivia's shoulder at Scott. "Oh. Sorry. It was last minute. Carla and Trent lost their photographer the other day, so they got Scott instead. He's just going over the event spaces with them to ask about placement and such. He won't be hanging around for long."

Olivia took a deep breath and glanced at him again. It was supposed to be a quick look, but she had to drag her eyes away from his handsome, sculpted features—high cheekbones, strong jaw, supple lips, striking amber-brown eyes. He was smiling down at Carla, the bride-to-be, in a way that was guaranteed to make any woman between fifteen and seventy-five breathless.

It might have even made Olivia breathless had she been hit by it unexpectedly, but she was immune to Scott's charms.

And he never smiled at her like that anyway.

Every smile he gave her was an implicit challenge.

"Stop glaring at him," Laura said with a mild eye roll. "He's the best event photographer in the area, and we have to work with him sometimes."

"I know. I just like to be prepared before I run into him so I can paste on my civil smile."

Olivia was usually good at civil smiles and charming small talk. She was better with people than any of her three sisters since Laura had a brusque way about her that some found intimidating, Penny's artistic nature drifted toward absentminded eccentricity, and Rebecca was sometimes shy. Because she had social skills and a way with words, Olivia had taken on all the public relations aspects of Holiday Acres as well as handling advertising and marketing.

She'd gotten a marketing major at the University of Virginia and had immediately come back home to work for the family business since her father had died around the same time she graduated and they'd needed all hands on deck.

Olivia loved her hometown. She loved Holiday Acres. And she loved almost everything about her job.

She didn't love Scott Matheson, however, and she wished she wasn't so hyperaware of his presence.

She could feel him—some kind of intense masculine energy radiating off him—even when her back was to him.

It was incredibly annoying.

She tried to ignore the tingling awareness and instead focused on Laura and her clipboard as they continued around the huge, picturesque barn that was part of the Holiday Acres property and used for events like banquets and weddings. She wished she had her sister's ability to focus on work no matter what.

Olivia had never been like that. She enjoyed her work, but her priority had always been people. So her thoughts kept drifting back to Scott.

Thirty years ago, her father had opened Holiday

Acres as a Christmas tree farm, and the business had grown over the years to include a dozen cozy rental cottages, a coffee shop and bakery, the barn and gardens for events, and the Christmas shop, which was so huge now that it had become a tourist destination. When her dad had died five years ago, she, her mother, and her sisters had taken on the business. Her mother died eleven months ago after a yearlong struggle with cancer, and Olivia and her three sisters were managing Holiday Acres now.

"Olivia? Can you come here a minute?"

Olivia turned toward the voice, which she recognized as belonging to Carla. Unfortunately, that meant she had to turn toward Scott as well.

She prepared a cool, unconcerned smile as she faced him, taking a mental inventory of her appearance at the same time. If she'd known she'd be seeing Scott today, she would have put on something more stylish and professional. As it was, her thick black leggings, soft red sweater, tall boots, and handmade infinity scarf were comfortable and flattering but too casual for a Scott outfit. She'd gotten her hair trimmed and highlighted last week, so it swung around her shoulders in a shiny golden-brown fall. She always did her makeup and nails, and the couple of winter pounds she'd put on this season were well hidden under her sweater.

Her appearance wasn't ideal, but it would do.

"Did you need something, Carla?" she asked, avoiding Scott's eyes although he was standing right there.

"We want to take some photos in the cottage if that's all right."

Carla and her fiancé had rented out one of their best cottages for their wedding weekend. "Of course," Olivia said warmly. "The Mistletoe Cottage will make lovely photos."

"Can Scott get in it for a few minutes today so he can scope it out beforehand?"

Olivia forced her eyes over to Scott's face, and she fought an immediate wave of attraction.

More than attraction, really.

Lust.

Hot, unadulterated lust.

It was so incredibly annoying.

"Of course he can," Olivia said smoothly, shifting her eyes back to Carla. "The couple who had booked it canceled because of the weather, so it's empty right now. But he's done a number of events at Holiday Acres. He's probably been in the cottage before." She was speaking of him in the third person on purpose. It took strategy to deal with a man as obnoxious as Scott Matheson, and even the small details mattered.

"I've been in the pink cottage and the animal cottage and the one with all the... Christmas doodads." His tone was edged with an arrogant amusement that made her want to snap her teeth. "Is this one of those?"

"No," Olivia gritted out. Their cottages were all warm, lovely, and tastefully decorated, and Scott had just made them sound tacky. On purpose. "This one is different."

"Then I'll need to see it if it's not too much trouble." The corner of his mouth had turned up, bringing attention to the sensual line of his lips.

Olivia had to force her eyes away. "Of course it's not too much trouble." She searched the room automatically for Rebecca, who'd always handled errands like this. But her younger sister had left this morning.

Rebecca was going to cooking school in Richmond, and she'd also just gotten engaged. Olivia was very happy for her sister, who deserved all the joy she could get, but she missed having Rebecca around all the time, and it would have been nice if Rebecca's fiancé wasn't Scott's younger brother.

It tied their families together even more than they already were.

The Holidays and the Mathesons shared a deep, conflicted history. Jed Holiday and Scott's father, Caleb Matheson, had been best friends until the two men had gotten into a huge fight seven years ago that had turned into a long-standing feud about Jed having cheated Caleb's father out of a share in Holiday Acres. Jed denied it, and Caleb was a hard, unfriendly man, so most of the community sided with the Holidays in the feud. After the men died (in a tragic accident that killed both of them), it was discovered that Caleb had been right and Jed had indeed cheated his father. So the sisters and their mother had tried to make up for it by offering all the surviving Mathesons a share in the business. At first only Russ, Caleb's brother, had taken them up on the offer. All three sons had refused. Then earlier this year Phil had finally relented when he'd gotten together with Rebecca.

Now only Scott and his older brother, Kent, were holding on to bitterness and resentment over the family conflict. For years after their fathers first fought, Scott had never encountered Olivia without saying something cutting and sarcastic, as if she personally were to blame for what her father had done. After a while, the sharp words transformed into mockery, as if he was always silently laughing at her.

As far as she was concerned, that was just as bad.

From what she'd observed growing up and what Rebecca had told her recently, Caleb Matheson hadn't treated his sons well. So perhaps Scott had reason for a dubious personal life.

But Phil had had the same father, and he'd managed to become a decent person. She wasn't sure why Scott couldn't do the same thing.

"Let me finish this up, and I'll take him out to see it in a few minutes." Olivia was still talking to Carla rather than Scott.

"I can go by myself if you'd rather." Scott was smiling in that smug way he had. He was laughing at her behind his amber eyes. He knew she was trapped, and he was enjoying it.

Olivia tried not to growl at him. "No. The cottage is locked. I'll have to take you. Just give me a few minutes."

She held on to her fake smile until she'd turned her

back to him, and as she approached her sister, she met Laura's eyes.

Laura was laughing silently too but in a more sympathetic way than Scott. "You should really give up on hating him. He's not as hostile as he used to be. I don't think he's really angry anymore. And with Phil and Rebecca getting married, you're not going to be able to avoid him."

"I know. I don't hate him. I just don't like him."

"If you say so."

"I do say so. What are you insinuating?"

"I'm insinuating that you have a special resentment against Scott. You don't hate Kent the same way even though Kent is the one who really hasn't forgiven Dad and the rest of us for what happened. Scott still won't accept our offer of partnership, but he doesn't seem to hate us for what Dad did like he used to. Kent does."

"Yeah, but Kent is holed up in a cabin in the woods. He's not a cocky, womanizing asshole who goes around gloating and laughing at me all the time."

"That's just Scott's way."

"I know it's his way. I don't like his way. He's a user, and I can't stand that." She let out a sigh. "It's not just about the family fight. I can kind of understand him still resenting it since what Dad did ripped his family apart. But it was Dad's fault. Not ours. We did everything we could to try to fix it, and he still acts like he's too good for us. Plus I wouldn't like him anyway. I don't like men who treat women the way he does."

Laura frowned. "I've never heard of him mistreating women. He just dates a lot of them."

"He goes through women like they're paper cups, using them once and then discarding them."

"Yeah, but he never makes promises to them or—"

"You think that makes it okay? I feel so bad for all the silly girls who gaze at him with stars in their eyes, daydreaming of being the one woman who will finally bring him to heel. They're so stupid, but I feel bad for them. They all end up crushed in the end, and Scott doesn't even care."

"Maybe he does care."

"If he does care, he'd stop sleeping his way through the three surrounding counties. He doesn't care. He's an asshole."

Olivia generally considered herself a nice, understanding person who knew how to empathize with other people.

But she had no pity for Scott Matheson. He seemed to exist for no other purpose than to infuriate her—and he enjoyed that fact.

"Okay," Laura said with another slightly amused smile. "If you say so. Russ says—"

"I don't care what Russ says." Olivia didn't normally speak sharply to her sisters, but her emotions had been strained by the encounter with Scott. "You might think he's God's gift to creation, but I don't."

Laura blinked, clearly taken aback. "What? What do you mean?"

Russ Matheson was Scott's uncle. He was only in his midforties since he'd been significantly younger than his brother, and he had worked in finance for a big company in Richmond for most of his career. But after Laura had discovered their father's lying and cheating, he'd been the first of the Mathesons to forgive and reconcile. He'd been working with them at Holiday Acres for almost four years now, and Olivia wasn't blind to how in sync Laura was with him.

But Laura was clearly oblivious to anything deeper than a business partnership with Russ, and she was openly shocked by Olivia's insinuation.

Olivia immediately felt bad about it. "Sorry. I didn't mean to be rude."

"I know. Scott always riles you up that way. But what did you mean about God's gift?" Laura's brown eyes were wide and bewildered. "He's a good guy under all the sarcasm. Tommy adores him." Tommy was Laura's six-year-old son, the product of a one-night stand. "But I don't think he's God's gift."

"Of course you don't." Olivia smiled at her sister, wondering if Laura was ever going to open her eyes. "I was just talking."

"Okay."

"I've got to show Scott the Mistletoe Cottage in a minute, so let's finish this up."

Laura immediately got back down to business. She was good at that.

Twenty minutes later, Carla and her mother had left Holiday Acres since the snow was getting worse and they didn't want to get stuck. Olivia killed some time after they left since she wasn't in a hurry for alone time with Scott and she liked the idea of making him wait, but eventually she had to give up.

The snow was coming down thick and fast now. If she didn't get Scott to the cottage soon, he'd be stranded in the main farmhouse with them for who knew how long.

That wasn't an acceptable scenario.

It didn't snow very much in this part of Virginia, and whenever it came down like this, the whole community shut down to wait it out.

Olivia found Scott lingering in the entryway, looking at something on his phone. He wore a black overcoat that was hanging open over his jeans and sweater, and he looked ridiculously sexy, even in so many clothes. He straightened up when she approached.

"Ready?" he asked with an arch of his dark eyebrows.

"Yes, I'm ready now. I can just meet you at the cottage so you'll have your car and can leave right from there."

"Sounds good to me."

Olivia put on her stylish gray wool coat with gloves and a stocking cap before she walked outside. She stopped abruptly. "Shit. It's snowing really hard now."

"We can take my SUV if you want. I've got four-wheel drive."

Olivia frowned. "We've got four-wheel drive too. I'm sure I'll be fine."

She had to wade through several inches of snow as they walked toward the private parking lot reserved for staff and family, separated from the large public lot. Once, she slipped on the wet snow and would have fallen had Scott not reached out to catch her. His hand was warm and strong, even through her coat and sweater.

The shiver she felt was from the cold. It wasn't from his touch.

It couldn't be from his touch. That would be too wrong.

The Holidays owned a pickup truck and a four-wheel-drive SUV that they used for work around the property. The SUV wasn't parked in its place, and Penny was getting into the truck.

Penny was twenty-nine, two years older than Olivia, and she was pretty in a messy, Bohemian way with reddish brown hair and a very curvy body.

Olivia waved at her sister until Penny rolled down the window of the pickup truck. "Where are you going?"

"I'm supposed to meet with Sheila Blankenship about those new nativity scenes she's carving," Penny explained.

"Maybe you should postpone until the weather is better. There's got to be five or six inches of snow already."

Penny made a dismissive gesture, looking blissfully unconcerned about practicalities like weather. She'd always been that way. "It will be fine."

"Do you know what happened to the SUV?"

"Laura just took it. She had to go pick up Tommy from his piano lesson."

Damn. That was both their four-wheel drives. And Olivia needed one right now.

"I'll be back in a couple of hours," Penny added.

"Okay. Be careful." Olivia was frowning, wondering if she should insist her sister stay home. It was one thing to drive around their own property in this weather. It was another to drive three towns away, especially for someone as scatterbrained as Penny.

"She shouldn't be driving out in weather like this," Scott said beside her.

Olivia stiffened. Maybe she'd been having the exact same thought, but that didn't mean she wanted to hear it from Scott. "She's an adult. She can make her own decisions."

"If you say so. You better ride with me though since your car isn't going to be able to handle the snow on the roads."

Olivia's car was a pretty little red sedan, and she knew very well Scott was right about it. She tightened her lips.

"You're not going to want to run off the road because you don't want to be in the same car as me. Even you aren't so silly." Scott's tone was lofty and amused, and it made Olivia want to hit something.

Or someone.

She'd been called silly and shallow all her life because she liked pretty things and she spent a lot of effort on her appearance. Her father had always patted her on the head and treated her like an attractive face was all she had to offer to the world.

She'd hated it then, and she hated it now.

"You're implying I'm silly about other things?" she demanded.

"I'm not implying anything. I'm cold and wet from standing out here in the snow, and as much as I like arguing with you, I'd rather get into the car."

"Fine." She felt huffy and impatient, and she took too big a step. Her foot slid on the slick snow on the pavement, and she almost went down.

Once again, Scott caught her, this time by putting both arms around her.

She fell against his chest and lost her breath at the feel of his lean body against hers.

Without thinking, she looked up at him and lost her breath again at the look in his eyes.

For a moment—just a moment—she thought she saw something warm and deep and soft there. She wanted it. Needed it. Leaned into it as her gloved hands tightened in his coat.

Then his lip curled up in his smug half smile. "If you want to hug me, you can do that too."

She sucked in an indignant breath and pulled away from him. "I wasn't hugging you. I slipped."

"I see."

"You were the one who hugged me."

"I get it."

"If you're going to be obnoxious like this, then you can

forget about getting into the cottage. I make a point of spending as little time as possible with arrogant assholes."

His smirk softened into a smile of genuine amusement. "That I know. I'll be as unobnoxious as possible."

"Good. So let's get going and make this quick. Because I suspect you can only make it a short time until your obnoxiousness rears its head again."

Scott laughed. "I suspect you might be right."

2

As soon as Scott got behind the wheel of his SUV, he started to worry.

The snow was still coming down hard. Harder than he'd realized. The roads were going to be bad, and people in this area weren't prepared for weather like this.

"Maybe we should wait," he said when Olivia settled herself in the passenger seat. "It looks pretty bad out here."

She shot him an impatient look, but he was used to that and knew it wasn't prompted by what he'd said. "You think so?"

"I don't know. Look at the roads. What do you think?"

"I think it's going to get worse if we wait. You want to spend the night here tonight?"

Scott always tried to keep his mind and body under control when it came to Olivia, but he was hit with a visual of himself in bed with Olivia—her lush, naked body beneath his, her long legs wrapped around him, her face twisting in pleasure.

The visual wasn't good for his state of mind. He tightened his hands on the steering wheel as his body reacted.

"I promise the floor of the barn isn't all that comfortable," Olivia added tartly. "But if you want to stay, you're welcome."

He took a deep breath and controlled himself. "All right. Let's do this then."

The parking lot was covered with snow, but it had been driven on and was mostly slush. And the private road that ran from the buildings and through the tree farm was straight and perfectly flat so he had no trouble driving it, despite the amount of snow piling up.

"I thought this snow was supposed to be only a few inches," Olivia said after a minute. She was sitting very stiffly in the passenger seat, and Scott didn't know if it was because she was nervous about the snow or because she disliked him so much. "This is way more than that."

"And you believed the weather forecast?" He didn't actually feel like banter at the moment since he was focused on the snow-covered road, but Olivia would expect it from him, so he tried.

"Not always." She obviously wasn't in a particularly argumentative mood right now either. Her tone was subdued. A bit tense. "But it seems like they should have known a snow like this was coming. It would have been nice to be prepared."

"Yeah. I'll only be a few minutes in the cottage. Then I'll get you back."

"You might be sleeping on the floor of the barn after all if the snow keeps up like this."

Scott should have disliked that idea, but he didn't.

Anything that kept him in the vicinity of Olivia excited him.

It always had. Ever since he'd been a shy, skinny kid with no social skills, and she'd been the prettiest, most popular girl in his class.

He'd never been foolish enough to hope in that direction, however. Not back then and not today.

He might believe Olivia was the best thing God had ever created, but she'd never believe the same about him.

When he realized she was still waiting for a response to her comment, he said, "I've slept in worse places."

"I'll bet you've slept in all kinds of places."

He slanted her a quick look and saw a faint scowl on her face. "You interested in all the places I've slept in?"

"No. Definitely not. I'm sure I don't have room in my mind for the enormous number of beds that would entail."

Scott chuckled at that, although his eyes were once again focused on the road in front of him. "I'm not sure it's as many as you think."

"It's a lot more than I have any desire to think about. You think girls don't talk about you afterward?"

Scott knew they did. And he knew they sometimes exaggerated—exactly as men would sometimes do. He'd had a lot of sex in his life—usually one- or two-night stands—but he wasn't the horndog the small town had painted him as for the past several years. A good number of the women he went out with he'd never had sex with. He only slept with women he genuinely liked and with whom he believed the good time would be reciprocal. He also didn't have sex with women who had marriage in their eyes. That limited his options considerably.

"You can't believe everything you hear," he murmured. "And that doesn't just apply to weather forecasters."

Olivia didn't answer, which was rather unnerving. After a few seconds, he slanted her a quick look to discover she was peering at him thoughtfully.

"What?" he asked.

"Who's made up stories about you?"

He didn't answer the question because he wasn't sure what she wanted to hear, and the truth would make him too vulnerable.

"Kelly Parsons?" Olivia asked.

Scott had to hide a cringe at the name. He'd gone out with Kelly once last year, and she'd come on to him very strong. He hadn't been into her, so he'd rejected her advances. They'd never had sex, and she hadn't taken it well.

The next week, stories were going around about how he'd made a lot of promises to her, screwed her senseless, and then left her high and dry.

It had bothered him a lot, but people would always believe what they wanted. There was nothing he could do about it.

He did like the idea that Olivia had immediately guessed one of the made-up stories, which seemed to prove she hadn't found the story believable to begin with.

"Scott?" Olivia prompted. "Was Kelly one who made up stories about you?"

"I'm not going to answer that."

When he shot a glance over, he saw she was looking annoyed, frustrated. He smiled, which made her scowl even more.

"Do you always have to be so infuriating?" she demanded.

"I do my best for you. I'm always trying to live up to expectations."

Her expression flickered briefly, which was worrying. Maybe she'd read an undercurrent in his words he never would have wanted her to hear.

He added, "After all, if you don't find me infuriating, no one will."

The question in her eyes disappeared in a familiar annoyance. "I know that can't be true. Most of the world must find you as infuriating as I do. How could they help it?"

Scott laughed, keeping his eyes on the road rather than letting them linger on her face. Her skin was clear, her eyes were blue, and her cheeks held a delectable flush at the moment. It wasn't just that she was pretty. It was that she'd always seemed to shine from within, as if something warm and vibrant inside her was peeking out around the edges of her features.

It was far too irresistible for a man to ignore, and it wasn't entirely fair that Scott was constantly slammed by the need to touch, to feel, to drown in that shining, when he'd never had even the slightest chance with her.

When they were twelve, she'd come into his garage where he was working on the model cars that he loved. He'd been so excited about her unexpected presence, especially when she'd asked a question about the cars like she might be interested in them.

But she'd just laughed at him and left, and he'd been crushed and mortified.

A fitting reflection of their entire relationship.

"You might be surprised," he managed to say, pleased his voice was as cool and dry as he always tried to keep it around her.

"I doubt it. I don't think anything about you could surprise me. Not since..."

Scott raised his eyebrows. "Not since what?"

"Not since you turned from a nice boy into an asshole that summer."

He knew immediately what summer she was talking about. The summer after they'd graduated from high school. Before they started college. They'd both been seventeen, going on eighteen. He hadn't seen her at all that summer, but they'd both started UVA in the fall, and they'd run into each other occasionally there.

He had changed that summer. In more ways than one.

He'd been an insecure loser all through high school. Then he'd changed. He'd become who he was now.

Whatever that was.

"You thought I was a nice guy at one time?" he asked, genuinely surprised by the idea.

"Of course I did. In high school you were always nice."

"You didn't even know I was alive in high school."

"Yes, I did. You sat near me in algebra and helped me sometimes. I thought you were nice back then. I'm not sure what happened to you, but you turning from that boy into an asshole was the only time you've ever surprised me. I liked you a lot better back then."

She appeared to be speaking the truth, and it made a knot of tension roil in his gut. He clenched his jaw and tightened his fingers around the steering wheel. "A lot has happened since then."

"I know it has. You think I don't know it?"

He darted her a quick look and saw from her face that she was talking about the feud between their families. That was something. It had changed him. But it wasn't everything.

Human lives were never shaped by only one thing that hurt them.

He didn't know what to say, so he didn't say anything. The snow was coming down even harder now, and he was having trouble seeing in front of him. When he turned off the road through the tree farm and onto the one that ran through the woods to the cottages, his wheels slipped. His heart jumped as he straightened out the car, finding enough traction to keep going.

Olivia had gripped the door handle as the vehicle slipped, and she was quiet now as he drove.

"This is terrible," she said softly after a minute or two of tense driving. "How did it get so bad so fast?"

"I don't know. But we're in the middle of the woods right now, so we have to keep going."

"I know it. We're not far from the cottage. It's not the next driveway but the following one."

"Okay. Good."

Scott held the car on the road as they plowed through the accumulating snow. If anything appeared in front of them, he'd never be able to see it through the snow, even with his wipers going full blast.

It might have been nice if he could pick up his speed a bit and impress Olivia with his driving skills, but ego always had its limits, and one of his limits was putting someone in danger.

He wasn't sure anyone else would be able to go any faster than he was going right now anyway.

When they finally reached the drive that led up to the cabin, he slowed down enough to make the turn without applying the brakes, hoping to avoid any more slips.

It didn't do any good. The driveway hadn't been driven on since the snow started, and it was thick and high and very wet. His tires pushed through it, landing on a layer of what felt like ice beneath it. With no traction at all, his SUV rolled right off the road, ending in the piled snow of a ditch.

The car jerked to an abrupt stop.

"You okay?" he asked, turning to Olivia quickly.

"Yeah. Fine. Fine." She rubbed her face with her hands, like she was trying to wake herself up. "No damage done. Not even to your car, I don't think."

"No. I don't think so." He put the car in reverse and tried to pull out of the ditch, but it was hopeless. His wheels spun and kept spinning. He put it in drive and then reverse again and tried to rock back and forth to find some traction, but it didn't do any good.

"Oh, just forget it," Olivia said after a minute. "This car isn't going anywhere for a while, and I'm not about to get out there and push it. We can just walk up the driveway to the cottage." She was already unbuckling her seat belt and securing her knit cap on her head.

"It's nasty out there."

"I can see that. But I'm not going to sit for several hours in this car with you when there's a perfectly good cottage a short walk away."

He couldn't argue anymore because she was already getting out of the car, and he knew she was right anyway. Walking in the snow wouldn't be any fun, but it would be foolish to let themselves get stranded in this vehicle for who knew how long when they had a better option.

He buttoned his coat all the way and put on his gloves before he pushed open his door and got out. The snow came halfway up his shins. He wore hiking boots, but they weren't nearly high enough to protect his jeans. They were soaked almost immediately.

He made his way around the car through the snow and

wind to find that Olivia had stumbled her way up to the driveway. When he reached her, he asked, speaking loudly to be heard through the weather, "You ready?"

"Yes, I'm ready. I'm capable of walking through a little snow, you know."

"Then let's go."

It was slow going. Very wet and cold and uncomfortable, on top of the effort it took to walk through so much snow. Olivia was doing well, but after a few minutes she was falling behind, so he slowed down and put an arm on her back to help her.

She jerked away from him, as he should have known she would. The jerk was a mistake. Her feet slipped out from beneath her, and she ended up falling backward into the snow.

It happened too quickly for him catch her, although he reached out for her instinctively as she fell.

"Damn it!" she burst out. She'd caught herself with her hands behind her, so she'd mostly landed on her butt.

"You okay?" He leaned over her, his heart racing from effort and surprise and tense anxiety and something else that always happened to him when he was close to Olivia.

"Yes, I'm okay. If you hadn't grabbed for me, I wouldn't have fallen."

He frowned. "I didn't grab for you. I was trying to help. If you hadn't jerked away from me, you wouldn't have fallen."

"You surprised me." Her cheeks were bright red, and snow kept landing on her damp skin and loose hair. She looked beautiful and angry and utterly delectable. "I wasn't expecting you to touch me."

"Well, I wasn't making a move on you if that's what you're afraid of."

"I know you're not making a move on me. I'm not that stupid."

She evidently thought he'd never dream of making a move on her, which meant she had no idea how much he struggled to contain his attraction for her.

That was good.

That was better.

That was safer.

He would hate it if she knew.

"I'm going to help you up now, so I'm going to touch you again." His tone was sharp and edged with disdain, and he knew it would make her angry. "But I'm not making a move on you, so don't jerk away from me again unless you want to land on your ass again."

He reached out both his arms to help her up, and she accepted the support, although she was so angry she was practically gnashing her teeth at him. As soon as she was back on her feet, she pulled her hands away from him.

"You're an asshole," she snapped, straightening up and turning to face the cabin again.

"I know that. But this asshole is all you have at the moment, so you're stuck with me."

"I might be stuck with you, but I don't have to like it.'

"I never expected you would."

There was something unexpectedly poignant about

the last words as they left his lips. Something he hadn't expected to hear in his voice.

He was briefly afraid it might reveal something he'd never want Olivia to know, but she was already marching toward the house again, and the words were lost in the snow and wind, blowing away in the frigid air with a flurry of flakes until it was like he'd never spoken them at all.

3

Olivia's hands and face were numb, and her leggings were soaked when they finally reached the door to the Mistletoe Cottage.

The small cabin was their honeymoon accommodation—a bitter irony right now given that it was Scott Matheson standing beside her, waiting for her to enter the code in the keypad to open the front door.

Scott was the last man in the world she wanted to be sharing a romantic cottage with, but at the moment it was their best option since otherwise they'd be stuck in the car or the snow.

Either one would be worse.

It took her a minute to punch in the master code that opened all the cottages since her hands were trembling and her eyelashes were caked in snow. She got the door open at last and stepped inside, leaving room for Scott behind her.

He shut the door with a loud sound, closing out the snowstorm and leaving them alone in a cottage that was made up of a large living area with a small, upscale kitchen against one wall, a dining area for two, and an oversized couch in front of a stone fireplace. She couldn't see it from where she stood, but she knew the one bedroom boasted a huge, luxurious bed, and the bathroom was gorgeous with a tub for two and marble countertops.

It was a lovely, comfortable, and romantic setting. She shouldn't be here with Scott.

Trapped.

Stranded.

Alone.

For who knew how long.

She stood shaking and hugging herself as she tried to process this reality.

"Don't just stand there in your wet clothes," Scott muttered from beside her. "You're going to freeze to death."

She shot him an annoyed look, but she was too cold and dazed to pair it with any words. She pulled off one of her wet gloves as Scott went to check the thermostat on the wall of the main room.

"I'll turn it up high until we get warm," he said. "As long as the power doesn't go out, we'll be fine here until the roads clear up some."

Fine.

He thought they'd be fine here.

Trapped with Scott Matheson in the Mistletoe Cottage in the middle of a snowstorm.

Sure.

It was all just fine.

Nothing could be finer in the world.

"What the hell, Olivia." He'd come back over and was standing right in front of her now. "Are you okay?"

"Of course I'm okay."

"Then take your clothes off and warm up." His face was handsome and tense and impatient. For some reason it made her shiver even more than she was already shivering.

"I'll take my clothes off when I want to take them off. You don't get to tell me when to do it."

"For God's sake, this isn't the time to be stubborn." He grabbed one of her hands and started pulling off the glove she hadn't yet removed. "Shit, your hands are freezing."

He rubbed them between his much bigger, much warmer ones, and the touch felt good. Really good. It warmed more than her hands. Her breath hitched in her throat at the sensations pulsing out from his hands against hers.

When she realized how good it felt, she yanked her hands away. "I'm capable of warming up my own hands."

"Then do it. Take your clothes off, or I'll take them off for you."

"Asshole." She said it out of principle because she knew he was right about getting warm. She couldn't stop shivering.

She took off her coat, hat, and boots and dropped them on the wood floor of the entryway. Then she went over to stand next to one of the heating vents to get as much warm air as possible.

"Your pants and sweater are wet too," Scott said. He'd removed his coat, boots, and sweater and wore nothing but a T-shirt, wet jeans, and wet socks.

"So? Yours are too. I don't have anything else to put on, and I'm not going to go around in my underwear, no matter what fantasies you might be indulging."

She didn't actually believe Scott had fantasies about her in her underwear. He'd never made any sort of move on her, and she assumed he never would. But it felt like something she should say, so she said it.

He gave her a curious look. "Believe it or not, having sex with a woman who can't stop shivering isn't one of my fantasies, no matter how hot she happens to be."

The words were so dry it took her a minute to realize he'd given her a compliment. Did he really think she was hot?

He added, "Doesn't this cabin come with amenities like warm blankets? And maybe extra clothes?"

"Oh. There are the bathrobes. They're really nice and warm. We could put those on and get out of our wet clothes." Her teeth were chattering, so it took a while to get the words out.

"Good. Let's do that. But you should take a hot shower first. You're still shivering, and I don't like it."

"I'm sorry you don't like it, but I can't help it. Not all of us are so hot-blooded we don't even get cold in a snow-storm. You don't have to be rude about it."

He was scowling now. "You can stop shivering by taking a shower." He strode into the bathroom and was in there for a minute before he came out. Then he walked over to her, put a hand on her back, and pushed her forward. "Get moving. Shower now. Argue with me later."

"I can argue with you and shower at the same time." It wasn't her most clever of comebacks, but it was all she could manage at the moment.

He'd pushed her into the bathroom, and she saw he'd turned the water on in the big, beautifully tiled walk-in shower. "If it helps, I'll stand right outside the door so you can argue while you get warm. But either way, you're getting warm right now."

When he started to pull her sweater off, she swatted his hands away and took it off herself. "Okay. God, you're a bossy asshole. I'm getting in, so get out."

"Good. Don't get out until you've stopped shivering."

She was still scowling at him when he closed the door to the bathroom, and then she quickly stripped and stepped into the shower.

The hot water felt delicious against her chilled skin. She wasn't so frozen that the heat was painful, and she couldn't help but sigh in pleasure. Her hair was half-wet and half-icy, so she put her whole head under the water. She stood under the spray for a long time, enjoying the warmth and the strong pounding of the water spray.

She wondered what Scott was doing.

A memory from four years ago hit her just then. Shortly after Laura had discovered in some old paperwork that their father had in fact cheated the Mathesons, Olivia had gone to talk to Scott. Although they'd never been friends, they'd been in the same class all through school. She'd known him all her life, and it felt like her responsibility to apologize to him for her father's actions.

So she'd steeled her courage and gone to his house one evening. He'd answered the door in sweats and no shirt.

She'd been taken aback by how attractive she found his broad shoulders and toned abs, but she'd stumbled out an apology and rearticulated the offer they'd made him of a share in Holiday Acres.

He'd looked at her coldly as she talked. When she'd finished, he'd asked, "You think I want anything from you?"

Then he'd slammed the door in her face.

She'd driven home in tears, trying to remind herself that his family had been wounded by hers. It still hurt though.

It hurt again now as she remembered it, even though he hadn't been cold and angry with her like that in more than a year. He remained obnoxious, however.

More obnoxious than anyone else she knew.

He sure had been bossy earlier about her being cold, but maybe he was the kind of guy who snapped into urgency in any sort of crisis—even if the crisis was just a little shivering.

Surely this snowstorm wouldn't last very long. Most snows in this area lasted only a couple of hours and melted off the next day. She wasn't going to be stuck with him in the cabin for days.

Probably just a few hours.

She'd be back in her own room and away from his obnoxiousness by the end of the day.

Hopefully.

Please God. Don't let her be trapped here with him for very long.

She wasn't sure what she'd end up doing.

When she was warm and relaxed, it began to bother her that she was naked in the shower with just one closed door between her and Scott, so she turned off the water, dried off with one of the big, thick towels folded on the shelf, and then pulled one of the white bathrobes off the hook to put it on.

It might feel a bit weird to wear nothing but a bathrobe around Scott, but she was fully covered from her neck to her ankles, and there was no way in hell she was going to put back on her wet clothes.

She towel dried her hair as much as she could and pulled out a brush from her purse to get the tangles out. Since it would get on her nerves wet and loose this way, she pulled it into two braids.

They made her look girlish, but they'd keep her hair out of her way, and it seemed like a good idea to wear the most unsexy hairstyle she could think of right now.

Not because she needed to persuade Scott.

But because she might need to persuade herself.

There was nothing sexy between them, and there never would be.

Satisfied with her sartorial choices, she left the bathroom.

It was already much warmer in the main room when she stepped out, and she found Scott looking in the refrigerator. "There's food in here," he said.

"Yeah. We'd stocked it this morning for the couple who were supposed to have it for the next two nights, but they ended up canceling because of the snow."

"Well, it might need to be restocked before the next guests arrive if we're stuck here for too long and we need to eat some—" He broke off midword when he turned around and saw her. His eyes ran up and down her body, from her bare feet to her braided hair.

"What?" she demanded, immediately unsettled by the look. "You bossed me into getting into the shower. You can't be surprised that I did it."

"I'm not surprised." There was a hoarseness in his voice that was strange. Kind of exciting.

She brushed the thought away. "Since you're still wearing your wet clothes, you should go take a shower yourself. I know you might like to pretend to be some superman, but you're not, and you've got to be cold in those wet jeans."

"I am. I'll take a shower."

"Then do it."

He stood where he was for another moment, his eyes running up and down over her one more time. Then he made an odd little jerk and turned on his heel to walk into the bathroom.

When he'd closed the door, she went into the kitchen, opening the refrigerator to see what was in it. She knew generally what to expect, so she wasn't surprised to see the juice, milk, eggs, cheese, butter, strawberries, prepared salads and sandwiches, and a small chocolate cake.

In the wine cooler were white wine, champagne, bottled iced coffee, and several bottles of sparkling water, and in the cupboard were bread, cereal, crackers, cookies, chocolates, and two bottles of red wine.

All part of the amenities of the cottage.

If she was here for more than two hours with Scott, she was definitely breaking into the wine and chocolate.

She pulled her phone out of her purse and called Laura.

"Hey," Laura said, answering on the second ring. "Are you okay?"

"Yeah. I'm okay. Did you make it back home?"

"No. I'm at the Candy Cane Cottage."

"Is Tommy with you?"

"No. I didn't make it that far. But I just called and he's fine. He's going to stay with Mae in town until morning." Mae was the woman who gave Tommy piano lessons.

"So you're all by yourself?"

"No. Russ is here."

Olivia arched her eyebrows. "Russ is? What is he doing there?"

"I got stuck. In the snow. He came to help, but then we

couldn't get back. We're fine. It's all fine." Laura sounded a little flustered, which wasn't at all like her.

"Well, we're in the same boat since I'm stuck here at the Mistletoe Cottage with Scott." Olivia made a face to the empty room. "At least you like Russ."

"Y-yeah."

Olivia was intrigued by the slight stammer over the word, but she could hardly grill Laura about what was going on with Russ right now when Scott might come back into the room at any moment. "What about Penny?" she asked.

"I tried calling her but couldn't reach her."

Olivia immediately forgot about her own minor frustrations. "Oh shit. Do you think she's okay?"

"I don't know. I don't think we need to panic yet. She's not really as scatterbrained as she acts. She can take care of herself."

"But she was trying to drive in this snow."

"If she needed to stop, she'd stop. Let's give it a few minutes and try her again."

"Okay. Let me know the minute you hear anything."

Scott came out of the bathroom just then, wearing a white robe that matched hers and looking relaxed and far too sexy with his damp hair, bare feet, and slight five-o'clock shadow.

At least Olivia would have thought he was far too sexy if she hadn't been so worried about Penny.

"What's wrong?" Scott asked.

"It's Penny. She left before we did, and we can't get in touch with her."

Scott frowned as he came closer to her. "She was only a few minutes ahead of us. If she'd run off the road, we should have seen her."

Olivia let out a breath as she realized he was right. "That's true. But she could have gotten farther and then run off the road. What if—"

He reached out to put a hand on her shoulder. "Don't imagine the worst yet. She's probably just somewhere she can't answer the phone. If you haven't heard from her in an hour or two, then you can worry."

Despite the flurry of anxiety in her mind, his calm voice did make her feel better. So did the weight of his hand on her shoulder.

She met his eyes and was momentarily trapped by them.

Then she remembered this was Scott—Scott—and she stepped backward, pulling away from his hand. "Okay. I'll wait an hour or two before I start to panic." She looked around, searching for something to do. When she saw the big couch, she went over to it, pulling down a cashmere throw from where it was folded to wrap it around herself.

She turned on the television. "I guess we can just hang out and watch TV until we can get out of here. At least there's food if we need it."

Scott went into the kitchen and opened the cooler. "Do you want some water?"

"Yeah. Sure. Great."

He brought two bottles of water over, and she accepted one of them, keeping everything but her hand under the blanket.

"You're not going to share that blanket?" he asked.

Her eyes widened. "No, I'm not going to share it. Are you crazy?" She nodded to the shelf behind the couch. "Get your own."

He was smiling a little as he reached over her to grab another blanket, and the two of them decided on a show about historical mysteries on television to pass the time.

After about twenty minutes, Olivia checked her phone for the fifteenth time, murmuring, "I hope Penny is okay."

"I'm sure she's—" He broke off when a phone rang in the room.

Olivia scrambled for hers, but it wasn't the one that was ringing.

It was Scott's. "It's Kent," he said, looking surprised as he answered the call. "Hey, what's up?"

He listened to whatever his older brother was saying for a minute. Then he met Olivia's eyes and said, "Penny is okay. She's at Kent's. She lost her phone in the snow."

"Oh, thank God." Olivia was almost slumping in relief as she hurriedly texted Laura and Rebecca to let them know.

Scott listened to his brother some more and then was almost smiling as he said, "Well, it's not her fault she's stuck there, so try to be nice. Let us know how you're doing." After another pause, he must have been answering a question from Kent when he said, "Olivia... Yes. ... Shut up. ... Be nice to Penny."

He hung up then.

"What was he saying?" Olivia asked, curious about the end of the conversation that seemed to be about her.

"He was complaining about getting stuck with company. He's been a hermit lately."

"I know he has. I'm sure Penny can handle it though."

"Yeah. I'm sure she can." Scott sighed. "Well, it could be worse. We've got heat and food and a television, so at least—"

His words were cut off when there was a weird crackle in the air. The lights all went off.

So did the heat.

"Shit," Scott said.

"You jinxed us."

"I was just saying—"

"You jinxed us!"

"Shit. It looks like I did."

Now this situation wasn't quite so comfortable. She was safe but still with Scott. And there wasn't any heat or light or television.

She had no idea what the hell they were going to do for the rest of the day.

4

SCOTT SAT FOR A MINUTE AFTER THE POWER WENT OUT, waiting breathlessly to see if it might come back on.

They lived in a rural county, and power problems happened fairly often in bad weather. The electricity would sometimes flicker but come back on within the minute.

He and Olivia both sat there on the couch in front of the cold fireplace and the blank television, but the lights didn't come back on.

"Shit," he muttered.

"Yeah." Olivia sat up straighter on the couch, letting her blanket fall down to her lap. "I guess it was too much to hope that we'd have power while we were snowed in."

"We're not that lucky, I guess."

"I guess not."

Scott stood up, feeling underdressed in the robe now that they weren't just sitting on the couch. "We should make a fire. It's going to get cold in here pretty quick." It was already significantly cooler in the room now that the heat pump was no longer blowing out hot air.

"Yeah. I can make the fire. Maybe you could go check the breakers just to be sure it's not a problem with our box."

Scott frowned at her. He might not be at his best at the moment in a robe and wet hair, but he was certainly capable of making a fire. "I can make a fire."

"I'm not saying you can't. I was just saying I could make it—"

"Why shouldn't I make it?"

He might not be as outdoorsy as his brothers, but she was acting like he was so incompetent she needed to make the damn fire for him.

It would have been nice if she'd see him as capable, but obviously she didn't.

A strange succession of emotions flickered across Olivia's face before she burst out, "Oh, for God's sake! You men have hardly made it past cavemen." She pitched her voice low and gruff to add, "Me big man. Me make fire. Me have big dick. Look at big dick and tremble."

Scott was momentarily torn between annoyance and amusement, and he ended up making a choking sound that might have been both at once.

She rolled her blue eyes. "You be a big man and make the fire. I'll check the breakers."

He thought that was a perfectly reasonable decision, so

he was confused when she strode over to the entryway and started putting on her boots.

He watched for a moment to confirm what she was doing. When she'd gotten them on, she pulled on her coat, which was still quite damp from the snow.

"What are you doing?" he asked.

"I'm checking the breakers. You be a big, strong man and stay inside where it's safe and warm."

He watched in astonishment as she swung open the door, letting in a gust of frigid air and a lot of blowing snow. Then she disappeared outside.

He ran over to the door after her, starting to follow until he realized he wasn't wearing any shoes. "Olivia!" he shouted into the wind. "What the hell are you doing?"

"I'm checking the breakers! What the hell do you think?"

It was only then that his mind started to work again. The breaker box must be in the storage room, and the only entrance was from outside.

And he—very stupidly—had let Olivia go outside to brave the snowstorm while he stayed safely inside in a robe and bare feet. "Damn it, Olivia!"

He could see she'd made it into the storage room. She left the door hanging open as she went inside. He hung out the front door, his feet freezing in the cold air and blowing snow, and waited until she reappeared.

"It's not the breakers," she called out, closing the storage room door and then hurrying clumsily through the snow toward him.

She was moving so quickly that she barreled into him. He caught her and pulled her inside, slamming the door behind them. "Damn it, Olivia," he said again, this time in a mutter.

She was gasping and shivering, but her eyes were laughing as she gazed up at him. "What? You wanted me to check the breakers."

"I didn't know they were outside!"

"Well, they were. You wanted to make the fire like the caveman you are, and you've done a pretty pitiful job of it so far, I'm sorry to say." Despite her light tone, her teeth were chattering as much as they'd been earlier when they'd first gotten to the cottage.

"Damn it, Olivia." This time the words were stretched and soft, spoken in absolute frustration.

"How many times are you going to say that?"

"As many times as I need to say it. Why the hell did you do that?" He hurried over to the fireplace, which was all prepared with three pretty logs arranged on the grate and more piled up next to the hearth. He grabbed a long match and some torn newspaper left for this purpose in a bowl, lit it, and when the paper was burning, tossed it into the wood.

"I did it because I was capable of doing it, just like you were capable of starting the fire." She'd come over to join him, rubbing her trembling hands in front of what was barely a flame.

Scott poked at the wood until the flame began to

spread. "Just because you're capable of it doesn't mean you should have done it. You were wearing a bathrobe!"

"I had boots on. And a coat." There was the slightest quiver in her voice that proved she was tempted to laugh.

Ridiculously, Scott was tempted to laugh too. "But no hat and gloves. You're shivering like crazy."

"Well, it's cold out there. And snowing like we're in Alaska instead of central Virginia."

"And I guess you would have gone out like that if we'd been in Alaska too."

"Maybe." She was slanting him the most delicious, shining look. It was making his heart do all kinds of flip-flops and making other parts of his body do gyrations of a different kind.

"Maybe." He was still poking at the fire, pleased that it was finally starting to blaze. "She tells me maybe."

"I'll tell you maybe when I want to."

"You think I don't know that?" He shook his head, trying not to smile. "Leave it to me to get stuck in a snowstorm with Olivia Holiday."

She frowned, some of her shining growing dim. "You could get stuck with a lot worse."

"You think I don't know that too?" Suddenly aware that he must be gazing at her like a sappy fool, he straightened up and turned his eyes away from her. "I've got the fire going."

"I see that." She was holding her hands out over the flames. She was still visibly shivering. "I'm going to see if my socks are still wet."

"Well, do it quick. Your hair is still wet, and you just stupidly ran out into the storm. You're going to catch pneumonia unless you warm up. I don't care how pretty you are. You can't go around doing things so stupid."

He felt more on solid ground now as he put down the poker. He picked up the blankets they'd been using from the floor and tossed them onto the couch.

After a minute, he looked over toward the entryway to see what Olivia was doing. She was still crouching down beside the wet socks she'd laid out near the heating vent earlier.

"What's the matter?" he asked. Something seemed different about her, although he could only see her back and so didn't know what it was.

"Nothing."

Her voice sounded like her posture. Something was wrong.

"What's going on?" he asked, walking around the couch so he could see her face.

She turned her face away from him. "Nothing. I just told you. What's your problem?"

His heart was racing again but for a different reason now. Something had happened in the past two minutes. "My problem is that I know something is wrong, and you're not telling me what it is."

She made an impatient sound and stood up, whirling around to face him and meeting his eyes with an expression that was clearly a challenge. "And this is the third time I'm telling you that nothing is wrong."

"I don't believe you."

"I don't care what you believe." Her eyes were narrow with resentment, but he could also see something else in her face. All her shining was gone.

It had disappeared. In two minutes.

And he had no idea why.

"Shit, Olivia, tell me." He reached out for her instinctively.

She jerked away from his hand like she'd been burned, and it told him something. She couldn't stand for him to touch her, and it was a lot more than her normal avoidance of him.

She was acting wounded.

Her shining was gone because of him. He was the one who had done it.

He'd done it to her before. He vividly remembered one evening four years ago when she'd come to his house to apologize for her father. He'd been hurt and angry and convinced she was just going through the motions, but he couldn't forget her face as he was slamming the door on her.

He'd wounded her. He still cringed when he recalled it.

No amount of hurt could justify it.

He wasn't going to do it again.

"Did I do something?" he demanded, sounding so urgent it was almost embarrassing. "I didn't mean to. Tell me so I can fix it."

"Would you shut the hell up?"

"I'm not going to shut the hell up until you tell me what I did. What's wrong?"

"The only thing wrong is that my socks are still wet!" She was completely in control of herself, her jaw tense and her spine perfectly straight.

But she wasn't shining anymore.

"Well, put them in front of the fire so they'll get dry," he growled, feeling so helpless and frustrated he sounded grumpy.

She walked stiffly over to the fire, laying her socks out on the hearth.

As he followed her, Scott searched his mind for what he'd said over the past five minutes. He'd been complaining about her going out into the snow, but it had just been their normal banter. He'd thought she was responding in kind.

"I'm sorry I yelled at you," he said, coming to stand beside her. "I was worried about you going out in the snow like that."

"I don't care if you yell at me."

That seemed to be the truth. He searched his memory even more. "And I really wasn't complaining about being stuck here with you. I was—"

"I know that." She sounded impatient.

"Then what the hell did I say? I didn't say anything except—"

"Except I was pretty," she burst out, as if she'd finally reached the limits of her control.

He stared at her in bewilderment. "But you are pretty."

That was so self-evident that it hardly needed saying. Anyone with eyes in their head could see it.

"I'm not just a pretty face. I'm not stupid."

Her voice broke on the last word, so he knew it went deep. He was drowning in confusion. "Of course you're not stupid. I never said you were stupid."

"You said I was pretty, making it sound like I was nothing but pretty. You said I was stupid for going out—"

"I did not say you were stupid!" He was outraged by the very idea. How could she possibly believe he would ever say or think something like that about her. "I'd never have said you were stupid. I said it was stupid to go out in the snowstorm in your bathrobe. I wasn't saying *you* were stupid. Am I crazy? I know how smart you are."

A tear slipped out of her eye that just about tore his heart out.

"Jesus Christ, Olivia, I'm really sorry. I didn't mean it like that. When I said I didn't care how pretty you are, I didn't mean because being pretty means you're stupid. I meant because you've probably always gotten your way, so you just do whatever you want, even going out in the snow without clothes on."

His embarrassingly earnest ramblings must have been getting through to her because the tension in her shoulders relaxed and her face softened. "I had a robe on. And a coat. And boots."

He let out a rough sigh. "I know you did. Shit, Olivia, I'm really sorry. I just thought we were doing our normal thing."

"We were."

"I didn't know you'd..."

"I'd what?"

"You'd get hurt."

She gave a little sniff and hugged her arms to her chest. "I wasn't really hurt. But I don't like to be called stupid and treated like I'm nothing but how I look."

"I didn't call you stupid. I'd never call you stupid. And I'm really sorry that I said anything that made you think I was."

"Okay."

"Okay?" The tightness in his chest was finally loosened as he realized he might have fixed things.

"Yes. I said okay. How many times do I have to say it?" Her tone was tart now, and her eyes were glinting a little, her shining finally starting to reappear.

"One more time." He couldn't stop the little smile curling on his lips.

She narrowed her eyes. "Okay."

His smile widened. "Good. I'm glad you're okay. I didn't think you'd ever get so emotional with me."

She stiffened. "I was not emotional. I was cold. I went out in the snow in my bathrobe."

Scott laughed out loud—in relief and genuine amusement and a new sort of excitement. "Well, if you're cold, then cover up and get warm."

He poked at the fire a few more times as Olivia climbed on the couch and cuddled up under the same blanket she'd been using before.

When he turned around, he grew still, staring down at her bundled body and beautiful, flushed face. Her hair was still damp and pulled into those ridiculous braids. Her eyes were way too big for her face. Maybe that was why she looked so vulnerable. Lonely.

"What?" she demanded, her teeth still chattering.

"Damn it, Olivia." He lowered himself onto the couch, and he simply couldn't help it. He pulled her against him, wrapping his arms around her and pulling the blanket up over both of them.

She didn't pull away. Just asked, "What are you doing?"

"You said you were cold, so I'm trying to get you warm. Do you have a problem with that?"

"No. I'd like to be warm again."

"Okay then."

She was soft and small and shivering against him, and she burrowed into his chest. He adjusted to get more comfortable, and she adjusted with him.

That sat like that, tangled up together in their bathrobes under the blanket until Olivia stopped trembling. She was relaxing now. He could feel it in her body.

It made him relax too. That might soon get dangerous, but he wasn't ready to let her go yet, and she wasn't pulling away.

"I'm really sorry, Olivia," he said after a long time. It was still late afternoon, but the snowstorm had hid the sun, and the room was dark except for the flickering light of the fire.

"You already said that."

"I want to say it again. I'm sorry enough to say it again."

"Okay. Thanks. I'm glad you weren't calling me stupid."

"I'd never even think such a thing. I know how smart you are."

"I'm not that smart."

"Yes, you are. You got good grades all through school, didn't you?"

"I did okay. Except in Algebra. You had to help me with that."

His hand was moving just a little of its own accord, making circles on her back. "I didn't mind. You did just fine. And you did well at UVA, didn't you?"

"Yeah."

"That's not an easy school. There's no way anyone could think you were stupid. Why would you even think that?"

"I'm not smart like Laura or talented like Penny or able to take care of everything like Rebecca. I've always just been... the pretty one."

"That's ridiculous. You can be pretty and incredibly smart at the same time."

He couldn't see her face since it was pressed against his shoulder, but it sounded like she was smiling. "I'm not incredibly smart. Don't get carried away with trying to make me feel better."

"I'm not trying to make you feel better. When have I ever tried to make you feel better?"

"Never."

"So there. It's true. I think you're incredibly smart. You

think I haven't seen what you've done for Holiday Acres since you've taken over the marketing and advertising?"

"Really?"

"Yes, really. Of course I've seen it. I know it's because of you. You're amazing." His hand was moving even more now—stroking up and down her back. He simply couldn't stop it. "Who the hell ever treated you like you were stupid and nothing but a pretty face?"

The question was a real one. He wanted an answer so he could strangle whomever it was with his hands.

It took a while for Olivia to respond. "Whenever I did something silly as a kid, my dad would shake his head and say, 'She's definitely the pretty one.'"

Scott had to hold back a growl with nothing more than the strength of his will. Their family history was too complicated and too fraught for him to put into words what he thought of her father. So he didn't. He thought it though.

"He didn't think I should even go to college. He'd always say a rich man was going to snap me up so why bother."

He couldn't hold back the growl any longer.

"I know," she said with a sigh, nestling against him in way that sent his head spinning. "He could be a real jerk. In all kinds of ways. But he loved me—as well as he knew how. And he was my dad, so I loved him."

"I know."

She lifted her head to look at him. "You do?"

He was gazing down at her, a pulsing growing in his

chest, his ears, his groin. "Of course I know. I know all about having a jerk of a father but still loving him."

She swallowed visibly. "I guess you probably do."

"At least you know your father loved you," he murmured thickly. "I have absolutely no way of knowing if mine ever did."

"Oh, Scott." She raised her hand to cup his cheek. "Of course he loved you. Your dad was raised hard, and he drank too much. He didn't treat you right. But of course he loved you."

"I... hope so."

They kept staring at each other. Her hand was soft and warm on his face. He had no idea what might have happened, but Olivia finally gave a little jerk and dropped her hand.

He thought she was going to pull away now, but she didn't. She laid her head back on his shoulder, reclining against his chest. She was between his legs now, and both his arms were around her.

This was a very dangerous position for the state of his body, but he wasn't prepared to give it up yet.

They were silent for a while, nothing but the crackling fire breaking the dark stillness of the room. Then she said out of the blue, "And I don't always get my way."

It took him a while to backtrack enough to follow her. "Maybe not always. But I guarantee you get your way a lot just because you're so pretty."

"I'm not that pretty. Not prettier than anyone else."

He snorted. "You're prettier than everyone else. You always have been."

"What do you mean?"

"I mean when we were nine years old, you wore pink ribbons in your hair for our school pictures, and I distinctly remember thinking that you had to be the prettiest girl in the world."

"You did not!"

"Yes, I did."

"I wasn't that pretty."

"Yes, you were. You're really going to argue with me about this?"

"I'll argue with you about anything I want."

"That has been made manifestly clear."

She giggled, and he couldn't help the prickle of pride at having made her laugh like that.

Then she said in a different tone, "Well, you're really good-looking. Do you always get your way?"

"Not always. But you've been pretty all your life, so you probably don't even notice when it happens. Whatever looks I have now, I definitely didn't have all my life. I very vividly see the difference in how people treat me."

She lifted her head to check his expression. "Is it that noticeable?"

"Yes. It's that noticeable. It's like I'm a different person now."

She was frowning. "Maybe you feel like a different person because you act like one. You're different now. You know you are. You used to be nice and shy and kind of..."

"Geeky? Clueless? Pitiful?"

"No!" Her mouth twisted. "You weren't really a geek. You liked all those model cars and didn't hang out with a lot of friends, but that wasn't what I was going to say. You were... sweet."

He let out a dry huff. "Sweet? Great."

"You were sweet. I liked it. Maybe that's why people treat you different now."

"If you say so. I'm definitely not sweet anymore."

"You're not going to get any argument about that from me. Although..."

His mind and body were still buzzing with excitement, and it was intensifying as the conversation grew more intimate. "Although?"

"You were kind of sweet before," she admitted, dropping her thick eyelashes. "After you hurt my feelings."

"You thought that was sweet?"

"Yeah." She lifted her eyes, and they were shining again. More than he'd ever seen before. "Kind of."

"I'll take it," he murmured.

There was absolutely no way he could resist anymore, even though everything in his brain told him to hold back the way he'd always done before.

He didn't hold back. He moved forward. He brushed his lips against hers.

The buzzing turned into a throbbing as soon as he felt her lips touching his. He leaned into the kiss, moving his mouth to feel hers even more.

Her breath hitched audibly, and one of her hands came

up to his shoulder. Then she was kissing him back, and it was better than anything. All her soft, warm shining burst out in visceral eagerness. Her tongue darted out to meet his, and he deepened the kiss, groaning low in his throat as his now full erection throbbed in pleasure, anticipation.

He knew he shouldn't be doing this, but there was no way to stop himself. His hand was moving now of its own accord, like it had been doing earlier. But this time it was slipping inside her robe so he could touch one of her breasts.

It felt exactly as he'd known it would. Soft and rounded and velvety smooth with a firm peak that tightened under his fingers.

He knew she liked how he was touching her. She arched into his hand and gave a little whimper against his mouth.

This was Olivia. Kissing him. Letting him touch her breast. He couldn't believe he was actually doing it. His vision blurred as he tried to process what was happening.

He'd wanted this for what felt like forever.

Maybe he'd been wrong when he assumed he'd never be able to have it.

5

Scott Matheson was kissing her.

He was *kissing* her.

One of his hands was on her breast and the other was holding on to her braid.

The surge of pleasure and excitement that rushed through her was like nothing she'd ever experienced before. She clung to his bathrobe, sliding her tongue against his, trying to get deeper, more of him.

Then one of the logs in the fire gave a loud crack, and the sound pierced the heated blur of her mind.

This was Scott.

Scott Matheson.

She wasn't supposed to be kissing him.

She wasn't supposed to even like him.

She gasped against his lips. Pulled back. Tried to straighten up from where she was sprawled on top of him.

He grunted when she accidentally kneed him in the thigh, but he let her go as she withdrew.

"What..." She tried to take a full breath, her face burning and her body still throbbing with want. "What was that?"

Scott looked just as flushed and dazed as her. He winced as he straightened up to a sitting position, adjusting his robe around him.

"What *was* that?" she asked again, a new kind of excitement rising inside her, one that had nothing to do with physical arousal.

Scott had kissed her.

He'd wanted to kiss her.

And the way he'd acted before the kiss had been... different. The conversation had felt special. Just as special as the kiss.

Maybe he'd felt that way too.

"That was a kiss," Scott said, his expression clearing like he'd managed to pull himself together.

She hadn't managed that yet. Her head and her heart might explode at any moment. "A kiss?"

"Yes, a kiss." He lifted his eyebrows just slightly with a glint of dry humor. "Didn't you recognize it?"

She stared at him breathlessly for a few seconds that stretched out far longer than they should.

He was back to normal. His typical irony—half teasing and half challenging. He'd been into the kiss for sure, but it must have just been physical if he was able to fall back into himself so quickly.

It had taken him less than a minute, and she was still barely able to get a word out.

Great.

Just perfect.

She'd gotten all excited about nothing.

There was no way in hell she was going to let him see it —not the foolish excitement or the crash of disappointment. She arched her eyebrows the way he was and did her best attempt at a cool look. "Uh, yeah, I'm capable of recognizing a kiss. I was wondering why it even happened."

"You were lying all over me and looked like you wanted to be kissed."

She gasped. "You're blaming this on me? You're the one who kissed me. I don't know what you're used to, but I don't go around kissing guys I don't like."

"Well, you kissed me, so what does that say?" He was still flushed, and he looked unusually tense, but his eyes were laughing at her.

Laughing at her.

He thought he'd won this encounter, and she secretly suspected he was right.

But she couldn't let him win.

She wouldn't.

"That says *you* kissed *me*."

"It was just a kiss."

"I know it was just a kiss."

"Then why are you making such a big deal about it?"

"I'm making a big deal because you kissed me just now,

and you're acting like it was just one of those things. I'll have you know, Scott Matheson, that I don't have any desire to be kissed by you."

Something flickered in his eyes, but it was gone before she could catch it. "You seemed to enjoy it just now."

"I was taken by surprise. I forgot it was you I was kissing."

That happened to be mostly true. She had forgotten it was obnoxious, womanizing Scott she was kissing. She'd been kissing a man who was funny and sweet and sexy as hell and softer than he ever let on.

She'd evidently been wrong.

"Well, it was me. So we can do it again if you want, or we can agree it was one of those things and let it go."

"I'm not going to kiss you again."

"All right then. So it was one of those things."

"Fine."

"Okay."

"Good."

She was breathing raggedly, her body still pulsing as if something was about to happen that she really wanted.

She was an idiot though.

This was what Scott did. He dated girls. He kissed them. He screwed them once or twice.

And then he moved on as if it meant nothing.

She wasn't going to be one of those girls.

She *wasn't.*

"I'm going to the bathroom," she said. It wasn't the best rejoinder in the world, but she had to say something.

Now that she'd said it, she needed to make herself move. She got up. Smoothed down her robe since it was gaping open in a way that showed too much of one breast. Then she managed to make her legs work enough to walk to the bathroom.

She shut the door with a loud click.

It was very dark in the bathroom. There was no window and no lights.

Damn.

She should have looked for a candle or a flashlight. Going back out now would feel like a defeat, however, so she fumbled her way to the toilet, sat down, peed, found the toilet paper in the dark, and then flushed.

She had to feel around for the sink so she could wash her hands. Then she splashed water on her face and stood for a moment, staring at the dark space where her reflection in the mirror should have been.

She'd wanted to kiss him. She'd wanted even more. And she knew he'd wanted it too.

But she wasn't going to be just another one-night stand for Scott.

She wasn't going to be a way to pass the time for him, a means of scratching an itch.

She wasn't a one-night-stand person, but she had nothing against them as long as both people understood what they were and were going in with the same expectations.

She obviously wasn't capable of controlling her expectations when it came to Scott, so she couldn't let herself do it at all.

It didn't matter how much she wanted to.

She wasn't going to do that to herself.

With that resolved in her mind, she felt her way to the door and went back out to the main room, where the fire was illuminating the space enough to see.

"It's dark in there," she said.

"Yeah. I just found a flashlight we can use." He was standing next to a drawer in the kitchen, and he switched on the flashlight in his hand. "Batteries work."

"Okay. Good."

"Do you need it now?"

"No. I already went. I'm capable of peeing in the dark."

"I guess we all have our talents." With that lilting comment, he took the flashlight into the bathroom and shut the door.

She scowled at the closed door for a moment before she went to the cupboard, pulled out a bottle of shiraz, found a corkscrew in the utensil drawer, and opened the bottle. She poured herself a glass and brought it over to the couch.

She'd need to replace the wine with her own money, but there were certain moments in life that required wine.

This was one of them.

She was sipping from her glass when Scott came back out. He stood in the middle of the floor, taking in what she was doing, and then he turned and went to pour himself a glass of wine too.

He came back to sit on the opposite end of the couch from her.

Neither of them said anything for a few minutes.

Olivia liked to talk. She liked to laugh and tease and share and understand other people. But she wasn't averse to silence sometimes, as long as the silence was a good one.

This wasn't a good silence. It felt tense. Uncomfortable.

Wrong.

When she couldn't stand it any longer, she burst out, "You really just go around kissing girls, no matter who they are?"

He jerked visibly. "Excuse me?"

"You heard me. I asked if you really go around kissing girls, no matter who they are."

"No. I don't kiss just anyone."

"Then who do you kiss?" She was pleased that her voice sounded casual since she felt anything but.

"I kiss..." He was looking at her in the orange light of the fire, and there was something odd in his eyes that soon changed into something laughing, more familiar. "I kiss women I want to kiss. And women who want to kiss me."

"And that's it. You kiss them. You screw them. And then you... just move on?"

"What else am I supposed to do?"

"Treat women like they're more than something to relieve your physical urges."

He stiffened. "I always treat women well. I never sleep

with anyone who doesn't want to sleep with me and who doesn't know my intentions. I never lead them on."

"And you really believe all the women you screw want nothing more than the one night you give them?"

"I tell them the truth. It's not my fault if they don't take me at my word."

She made a dismissive sound and matched it with a wave of her hand.

"What does that mean?" Scott demanded with a frown.

"That means you're being ridiculously naïve if you don't think some of the women you have sex with aren't hoping desperately that you'll change your mind and love them forever."

"I can't help what women are secretly hoping. They're human beings with minds and free wills just like me. If they don't want to have sex with me, they don't have to."

"They do want to have sex with you!" She blinked when she realized what she'd just said. Clearing her throat, she reworded, "I'm sure they do want to have sex with you. They just also might want even more, and a nice guy might realize that and not treat them like they're disposable."

"Disposable?" He'd been having this conversation with his typical ironic nonchalance, but now he sounded almost offended. "I don't treat women that way."

"Don't you? How many women have you slept with in your life?"

"Seriously?"

"Yes. Seriously. How many?"

"I-I don't know." He looked almost surprised by this admission.

"You don't know. You can't even remember. Do you remember their names? The color of their eyes? How they like to be touched? And you're telling me you don't treat them as disposable?"

She'd thought they'd been having one of their normal arguments, but he was reacting differently. He gazed at her for a long time, like he was baffled, disoriented. Then he said, "I don't... I don't think I've treated them that way. I could remember their names if I thought about it for a few minutes."

Then he appeared to be doing just that, going over the list of women in his past, trying to remember their names.

He looked so upset by her questions that she (irrationally) felt bad about it. So her tone was milder when she said, "I'm sure you didn't treat any of them badly. No one has ever complained about you except a couple of women I'm pretty sure never had sex with you at all. But part of seeing women as fully human is recognizing that women are all different—different from each other and different from you—so none of them are going to be approaching sex with exactly the same attitude you have. Sex is never going to be simple, no matter how much you try to make it so."

"I don't... I don't think it's simple."

"Don't you?"

"No." He met her eyes suddenly with an intensity she didn't understand. "I don't."

"Okay."

"And I didn't kiss you because I thought you were disposable."

"You didn't?"

"No."

"Okay then."

He kept looking at her in the flickering firelight. "Are you mad at me?"

"Not really."

"Did you really want to kiss me?"

The question was so vulnerable and so unexpected that she couldn't answer it with anything but the truth. "Yes. I wanted to."

"Good. I wanted it too."

They fell into silence again as they finished the wine in their glasses, and this time the silence wasn't nearly so uncomfortable.

It felt like they understood each other. Maybe for the very first time.

She wasn't sure what that meant. She'd never dreamed she'd feel connected to Scott this way. It was unnerving. Unsettling. Unbelievable.

She wondered if she'd ever be able to hate him again.

6

SCOTT FELT LIKE HE'D BEEN THROUGH A BATTLE, BUT IT HAD just been one short conversation with Olivia.

He had no idea how she was capable of doing that to him.

The past six hours had been an emotional roller coaster, and he wasn't likely to get off anytime soon.

He wasn't even sure he wanted to—not if it meant he could feel the way he'd felt when he was kissing Olivia, even for a minute, even with the crash that inevitably followed.

When he'd finished his glass of wine, he knew he needed to distract himself from Olivia's rumpled, half-dressed sexiness on the couch beside him. Even though she'd made it perfectly clear she didn't want him to touch her again, he was having trouble thinking of anything else. Her hair was still pulled into two braids. Her face was scrubbed clean—flushed and slightly dewy. Her graceful neck and the V exposed by her bathrobe were utterly irresistible. And her eyes were deep and knowing. Like she understood him. Like she saw deep inside him.

He shouldn't want her to. He shouldn't want anyone to know him that intimately. It left him too vulnerable, and he'd spent the past ten years trying not to be vulnerable again.

But he still wanted everything he saw in Olivia, no matter what it meant to his emotional safety.

He finally forced himself to get to his feet so he wouldn't reach out for her again. "I guess we should get something to eat. It's still snowing, so we're not getting out of here until morning at the earliest."

She cleared her throat. "Yeah. I guess so. There's stuff in the refrigerator that doesn't take any cooking, so at least we won't have to try to cook on an open fire."

They both went into the kitchen to peer into the refrigerator, pulling out the prepared sandwiches and salads and pulling out plates and utensils. They poured more wine and brought their food over to the couch to eat.

It was really good, and Scott enjoyed both the food and Olivia's company, even though they only made a few random comments as they ate. When they'd finished, Scott took the dishes back to the kitchen, rinsed them in the sink, and stuck them in the dishwasher, even though there was no power to run it.

Eventually the electricity would come back on.

Eventually he'd have to return to the real world from this intimate, intense firelit world he was stranded in with Olivia.

When he came back to the fire, Olivia was pulling her socks on. "They're finally dry. It feels like your T-shirt is too but not your jeans."

"I'll sleep in my shirt and underwear." He was still wearing his boxer briefs under his robe since they'd never gotten wet.

"Yeah. My tank is dry, and my leggings feel like they'll be dry in another hour or two, so I can sleep in them." She returned to the corner of the couch and stretched out, pulling the blanket up over her. "I wish we had a TV to watch."

"There are books over there." Scott lowered himself onto the other corner of the couch, extending his legs and covering up the way she was. The couch was oversized, so there was room for both of them to recline without more than the occasional brush of their thighs.

"I don't feel like reading."

"Me either."

Olivia closed her eyes, causing her dark eyelashes to fan out against her skin. "Maybe I'll just sleep away the rest of the day and when I wake up the power will be back on."

"You can give it a try."

She kept her eyes closed, but he knew she wasn't sleeping. He was relaxed now after the food and the wine. He wasn't aroused anymore since the confrontation that had followed their embrace had disturbed him enough that he'd lost his erection.

It could come back at any moment if given even the slightest provocation, but he would rather it didn't.

He didn't like that Olivia assumed he treated women as disposable. And he didn't like that a little part of him wondered if she might be right.

He also didn't like that kissing Olivia had cracked the foundations of his world.

There had been nothing casual about it, no matter how he'd tried to cover it afterward.

Kissing her had been... everything.

She hadn't felt the same way though. She'd been into it physically, but it had upset her. She didn't want to do it again. She didn't like casual sex, and evidently all she'd ever feel for him was casual.

He'd never believed she'd want him in any way, so he should probably be gratified that she even wanted him physically.

But he wasn't.

He hated it.

He wanted her to want him the way he wanted her.

But all she saw—all she knew of him—was what was on the surface, and that wasn't him at all.

Brushing the thought away, he made himself blow out the feelings with his breath.

"You remember when we were in sixth grade?" Olivia

asked out of the blue. Her face was relaxed, and her eyes were still closed.

"I remember some of sixth grade."

"That field trip to the zoo."

The memories came rushing back to him with a swell of conflicted emotions. "Oh. Yeah. I remember that."

"I was watching the sea lions and loved them so much I didn't want to leave them. So I was trailing behind and then went back to look at them one more time." She was smiling now, as if enjoying the memories. "Then I got left behind by the class."

"It was your own fault. The teacher told you three times to come."

"I know that. She thought I was following them, but I went back to give the sea lions one more look." She opened her eyes and smiled at him. "You were the one to come back to get me."

"I saw you weren't with us."

The truth was he'd always been hyperaware of her presence, even when they'd been kids, so he'd known immediately she wasn't with the rest of the class. He'd been conscientious back then. He'd been worried about her—more that she'd get into trouble than that something would happen to her.

She was still smiling, and her face had softened to that special, tender, shining look that felt like it was only for him. "And you wouldn't even talk to me!"

"I told you to hurry up."

"I know you did. You said hurry up. *Hurry up*. And that was it. Even when I tried to talk to you as we were catching up with the others, you wouldn't say anything to me. I assumed you thought I was an annoying, silly girl who couldn't follow directions and wasn't worth your time."

He huffed in amusement at how wrong she was. "That wasn't it at all."

"Then what was it? I tried to talk to you, and you wouldn't say a word to me but hurry up."

He shook his head, wondering if he should tell her the truth. It felt wrong to lie to her right now, to make a story up to protect himself. So he ended up admitting, "I was scared."

"Scared?"

"Scared."

"Of what?"

"Of you." He shook his head, smiling but avoiding her eyes. "Remember what I told you about thinking you were the prettiest girl in the world?"

"Yeah, but you said that was when we were nine. This was years later."

"So? You think anything had changed? You were the prettiest girl in the world, and everyone loved you and wanted to hang out with you. I was... clueless with people, particularly girls. I knew I would say the wrong thing if I tried to talk to you, so I didn't say anything."

She slanted him an adorable, laughing look. "You were shy." She said it as if making a brand new discovery.

"Yes, I was shy. I was petrified of girls. I was petrified of you."

"I had no idea. I just assumed you never really liked me and thought I was silly because I wasn't good at math and didn't care about all your model cars and everything."

"I never thought you were silly."

"Oh. I didn't know."

Scott was briefly uncomfortable, afraid he'd said too much, but she wasn't looking at him differently. She seemed as into the conversation as ever, so he hadn't revealed too much.

"So what changed?" she asked after a minute.

"With what?"

"With girls. How did you go from that shy little boy to..."

He arched his eyebrows. "To what?"

"To... who you are now." She waved her hand in his general direction, as if to take in everything about him. "How did that happen?"

"I don't know. I guess I just... grew up. Figured out I could be... I could be someone that women might want." He didn't like the stilted nature of his words, but he was doing his best to tell her the truth without telling her everything.

It was important to him that he not tell her everything. There were limits to how vulnerable he would allow himself to be.

"Oh. I guess that makes sense."

"Does it?"

"Yeah. I still think I like that boy better." She wasn't looking at him now. She'd closed her eyes again. "He was nice even if he wouldn't talk to me."

"That boy is long gone. And no matter what you say now, you never would have given him the time of day."

She frowned, meeting his eyes. "You have no way of knowing that."

"Yes, I do. I know him. And I know you. You barely even noticed he was alive."

She didn't argue. She couldn't argue. But the truth was perfectly clear.

Olivia was never going to give herself to him—not back then and not today. But at least she wanted to kiss the man he was today.

She never would have wanted to do even that if he hadn't changed from the boy he used to be.

She got up off the couch abruptly.

"What are you doing?" he asked, surprised by her sudden move.

"I'm going to make s'mores."

"Seriously?"

"Yeah. We have all the stuff here, and I'm not going to waste this fire."

Scott got up too. "Okay. Sounds good to me."

"You're going to make them too?"

He frowned at her. "Why wouldn't I?"

"I don't know. I just thought you'd be too cool for them or something."

"Weren't we just talking about how I'm not really cool at heart."

She laughed softly. "I guess so."

So they went to the kitchen, got chocolate, graham crackers, and marshmallows as well as metal skewers and dessert plates and brought everything over to the hearth. There, they sat down, skewered their large marshmallows, and toasted them over the fire before putting the s'mores together.

Olivia was giggling as she put her treat together, and she moaned in pleasure as she ate it. Scott couldn't tear his eyes away from her pink lips and her tongue sliding along her full mouth as she licked away melted chocolate and marshmallow.

He wondered if her face would look similarly when she was making love, that glow of pleasure and laughter and pure joy.

He did enjoy eating his s'mores, but he enjoyed watching her even more.

When they were through, they had another glass of wine to finish off the bottle, and then Scott went into the bedroom to build a fire in the fireplace there.

While he was doing that, Olivia went into the bathroom and emerged wearing her leggings, socks, and little white tank top.

She was obviously planning to sleep in the outfit, and it left nothing about her body to his imagination. He could see all of it. Her long legs. Her firm flesh. The curves of her thighs, her hips, her breasts. The way her stomach curved out just slightly with the most delicious softness.

He could see how soft it was. How soft she was. He wanted to touch her so much he had to tighten his hands into fists.

"What?" Olivia demanded. "I know it's kind of early, but what else do we have to do? I'm tired. I'm going to go to bed as soon as the bedroom warms up."

"That's fine with me. I can sleep on the couch. It's plenty big."

"You don't have to sleep on the couch." She looked surprised, almost offended by the idea.

"I don't?"

"No. Of course you don't. It's a king-sized bed, for God's sake. We're adults. It's cold outside, and there's no reason to keep both fires going all night. We can put a couple of pillows between us if you're worried I'm going to try to snuggle with you or something. We can both use the bed."

"Okay. That's fine with me."

She nodded, checking his face as if she couldn't tell what he was thinking.

That was just as well because what he was thinking was basically just a silent scream about sharing a bed with Olivia.

She wasn't inviting him to have sex. That much was clear.

He would need to make sure not to turn it into something it wasn't.

"I might take a shower first," he said, deciding he'd

need to make a few preparations before he got into bed with her.

"A shower? But it's going to be dark and cold."

"There should be enough hot water in the water heater for a quick shower. I won't be long."

"I don't care if you're long or not. You can do anything you want." She tugged her tank top down over her waistband, but it did nothing to hide the outline of her belly, her firm breasts.

Scott gulped.

He was definitely taking a shower.

The warmish water lasted the ten minutes it took for him to get under the spray, jerk off as quickly and silently as possible, and then soap up and rinse off. The bathroom was eerie with just the light of the flashlight, but it didn't bother him. He dried off, pulled on his white T-shirt and gray boxer briefs, and saw that Olivia had found a little sample tube of toothpaste.

There wasn't a toothbrush, but he squeezed some out and used his finger before rinsing out his mouth the way she must have done.

It was better than nothing.

When he came out into the bedroom, Olivia was already in bed, lying on her side, facing the fire which was blazing nicely now.

Her eyes were open, and she'd taken the braids out of her hair.

"Was the water still warm?" she asked.

"Yeah. It was fine."

He went to the other side of the bed and climbed under the covers beside her. "Did you want to use pillows?"

She rolled over to face him. "No. I don't really care. I know you're not going to make a move on me uninvited."

"Okay. Good." He rolled onto his side the way she was so he could see her.

They stared at each other for a minute.

"I feel weird," she said at last.

"About what?"

"I don't know. Just weird. Like my stomach is... uptight about something. But I don't know what about."

Her eyes were wide open. She was telling him the truth. She was a lot more honest about her feelings with him than he'd ever been with her.

"I feel kind of weird too," he admitted.

"I don't like the sound of the wind out there. And I don't like that it's so dark and quiet in here. It feels like we're alone in the world right now."

"I know. I feel that way too."

"I don't like it. It makes me feel... weird."

He wished she'd use a more specific word than weird. He was getting excited again—not physically but that pulsing in his chest he'd felt before.

She took a deep inhale and then let it out. "Do you mind if I..."

He frowned when she trailed off. "If you what?"

"If I get... closer to you? I don't like feeling like this."

The pulsing in his chest was totally out of control now. His voice was hoarse when he replied, "Sure. Sure you can. Get as close as you want. I promise not to make a move on you."

He moved toward her, and she scooted even closer until she was up against him. He wrapped his arms around her since there was no other way to make the position work. "Thank you," she murmured, nestling against him the way she had on the couch.

"Is this okay?" he asked, reminding his body that he'd just given it release in the shower earlier and it wasn't to get excited about the feel of Olivia against him.

"Yes. It's good." She took another deep breath. "I feel a little better."

"Good. Me too."

He was speaking the truth. His heart was still pounding out an intense staccato, and his body was really liking the softness and warmth and curves of hers.

But something else inside him was relaxing, softening, settling into comfort, security. Something he'd never realized had been out of sorts for a really long time.

"I'm glad I'm not alone in the snowstorm," she said after a few minutes.

One of his hands had moved up to stroke her hair, but he wouldn't let it move any lower than that. "Me too."

"Good night, Scott." Her body was relaxing even more. She was must have closed her eyes, getting ready for sleep.

"Good night, Olivia."

She was asleep in about ten minutes, but Scott didn't go to sleep.

He stayed awake for a long time, listening to the fire and the wind howling outside and holding Olivia in his arms.

7

Olivia woke up the next morning and didn't want to get up. She was warm and cozy under the covers, and the fire was still burning so Scott must have gotten up a couple of times during the night to tend it.

She wasn't cuddled up against Scott anymore, but she could feel his hot presence in bed beside her. When she turned her head, she saw he was asleep, one of his arms out from under the covers and stretched out toward the opposite end of the bed.

The power still wasn't working, but daylight was peeking in around the blinds.

She watched him sleep for a moment. Then she made herself get out of bed, no matter how shocking the cold air of the room. She needed to pee, and it wouldn't be smart to gaze at Scott sleeping for much longer.

She shouldn't feel so close to him.

She really shouldn't.

When she'd gone to the bathroom, she dug her brush out of her purse so she could comb her hair. It had dried in messy waves and flips, but there was nothing she could do about that.

She went to the big windows in the living room and looked out, relieved when she saw that the sun was out. It had stopped snowing sometime during the night. But everything in sight was covered with a thick layer of snow.

They weren't going to be getting out of this cottage very early today.

She'd kill for some coffee, but it wasn't worth the trouble of trying to boil water in the fireplace so she could use the french press. She settled for a bottle of premixed, sweetened iced coffee from the wine cooler.

She was freezing now, so she hurried back into the bedroom to discover that Scott was awake. He was still stretched out under the covers, but his eyes were open. "You want one of these?" she asked, showing him the iced coffee.

"Sure. That's better than nothing."

She ran back to get him one and then hurried to get under the covers.

"You're shivering again," Scott said, opening one of the bottles and handing it to her before he opened the other for himself.

"It's cold in the other room. But it stopped snowing and the sun is out. Hopefully we'll get a lot of melting."

"If it warms up enough, we probably will. And eventually they'll come by with snowplows."

"Chuck and Ed are really good about clearing the roads on Holiday Acres. They'll probably get to us by the afternoon. Even if the county roads aren't cleared yet, we'll be able to get out of this cottage."

"That's good."

She looked over to check his expression but couldn't read anything on his face. He looked ridiculously sexy with his rumpled hair, heavy-lidded eyes, and a day's worth of beard.

But she wasn't supposed to be thinking about that.

They drank their iced coffee in silence for a few minutes. Olivia was feeling warmer, more awake, and more relaxed at the same time.

Then Scott said into the silence, "Fifty-six."

She blinked. "What?"

"Fifty-six. My number. It's fifty-six."

Her eyes widened. "Fifty-six?"

"Yes. That's what I said." He wasn't meeting her eyes.

"You've slept with fifty-six women? Fifty-six?"

"Yes. I counted them up. I remembered them all." His eyes were utterly serious.

Bizarrely, she was touched by the admission, by the sobriety with which he was telling her. "You remember all of them?"

"Yes." His face twisted briefly. "I can't remember all the names, but I remember their faces, what they were like."

"How long did it take you to count them all?"

"A couple of hours."

"You did it in the middle of the night?"

"Yes."

She put down her coffee and rolled over to face him. "So you've slept with fifty-six women?"

"Yes. Over ten years. Fifty-six women over ten years. Do the math. It's not as many as you're thinking."

She did do the mental math, and he was absolutely right. If they were evenly spaced, he'd only slept with five or six women a year.

"I guess so," she said slowly. "You go out with different women so often I guess I assumed... it was a lot more."

"It's not. Most of the women I go out with I don't go to bed with."

"I didn't know that."

"I know you didn't."

She was breathing faster than she should be. She had no idea why. "I'm sorry. I didn't mean to... judge you like that."

"It's fine. I've done a lot that deserves judgment. I've tried not to be an asshole, but I've not always been great with women. You were right about a lot of things. Maybe fifty-six women sounds like a lot. Maybe it is. But, except for one, I only slept with them once or twice. I guarantee anyone who's been in a real relationship for more than a few months has had more sex than I have in their life."

She took a deep breath to try to slow down her heartbeat. It didn't work. "I've slept with five different guys."

"Five?"

"Yeah."

"But you dated Mike French for almost a year didn't you?"

"Yeah."

"And Tom Wilson for six months."

"Yeah. Something like that." She wondered how he remembered the length of her two longer relationships, but she didn't have the time to think it through.

"You had sex with them at least once a week on average?"

"Yeah. At least. Probably more."

"Then you've had more sex than I have."

It was such a new and unexpected thought that she had trouble getting her mind around it. She wasn't sure why it seemed to change things for her, but it did.

"Who was number five?" Scott asked in a different voice.

"Five? Of the guys, you mean? Tom was. Last year."

"No, I mean other than Tom and Mike. And I'm assuming Rick from high school and that football player in college. Who was number five?"

She told herself it wasn't surprising that he knew four of the guys she'd slept with since they were the four she'd had relationships with that lasted more than three months. But she still found it unsettling that he'd immediately known who four of them were.

But he didn't know number five.

Scott's amber eyes were deep and sober as he gazed at her. "You don't want to tell me?"

"It was Sammy. Sammy Shelton. From high school." She swallowed hard after she'd blurted out the words.

Scott lifted his head from the pillow and reached over to put down his empty iced coffee bottle. "Sammy?"

"Yeah. We went out for a few months on and off when I was sixteen."

"I knew that, but I didn't know... You had sex with him?"

"Yeah." She bit her bottom lip and then released it. "He was my first."

"Shit."

"Why do you say that?"

"Because he was a real asshole. He'd be a terrible first."

She sighed and admitted, "He wasn't as terrible as you might be thinking, but he wasn't great."

"What happened?"

"Nothing really. We went out several times, and I thought I liked him. What did I know? I was sixteen, and he was a senior and captain of the football team. If he liked me, then I wouldn't dream of not liking him back. At first we just kissed, but then he started to get more handsy. I knew what he wanted, and I wanted it too. I did. He didn't force me or even really pressure me. I knew what I was doing." She shook her head and closed her eyes for a minute. "It just wasn't what I thought it would be."

"Shit."

When Olivia opened her eyes, Scott was scowling at an empty spot in the air. "It was very uncomfortable for me, and Sammy didn't know how to make it better."

"I bet he didn't even try."

"He didn't try very hard. Then afterward he decided I wasn't good enough to bother with a second time. His exact words were..." She stopped, wondering if she should be telling Scott this.

She'd never told anyone. Not even her sisters.

"What did he say?" There was an edge to Scott's voice she didn't recognize.

"He said I was pretty but kind of immature. And I didn't know how to make a guy feel really good." Her voice broke with a pain that was years old now. "Of course I didn't know. I was sixteen and had never done it before."

Scott made a growling sound. "That asshole. The next time I see him around—"

"You'll do absolutely nothing! It's private, Scott. It's over. I'm a grown-up now. A lot of people don't have it really good for their first time."

She watched as the angry tension finally relaxed on his face.

"I might not have always been great with women, but I've never been like that. I hope you don't think I've—"

"I know you haven't, Scott. I know you'd never be like that. Even when I hated you, I never thought you'd... I know you're not like that."

To her surprise, his eyes glinted with a newly awakened humor. "So you don't hate me now?"

She gave an exhale of laughter. "I don't know if I'd go that far."

"Okay."

She reached over to finish off her iced coffee, and then she rolled over to face him again. "So what was your first time like?"

Something happened to his face. She saw it.

Stiffening in anxiety, she said, "Scott? What's the matter? Is there something bad about your first time?"

"No. No, of course not. It was fine. It was... fine."

"Then who was it?" She thought back to the overly friendly girl with braces that Scott had taken to the prom. "Heather? From high school?"

"No. Not Heather. I didn't have sex until I'd already graduated. I told you. I didn't know what I was doing with girls. I got a late start."

She frowned, trying to put pieces together. "So who was it then? Did it happen that summer? That summer you... you changed?"

His expression flickered again, and she knew the answer to her question.

She needed to know now. She *needed* to.

"Who was it, Scott?"

He looked at her. Didn't answer.

"You're really not going to tell me, after I told you?"

He cleared his throat and shifted position slightly. "I was helping out on the Lawsons' farm that summer. To make some extra money for college."

"Oh yeah. I remember that. That was after Mr. Lawson died, wasn't it?"

"Yes. It was just her. Jane."

Olivia froze. She didn't move—couldn't move—for several seconds.

"She..." Scott cleared his throat again. "She liked me."

"She liked you!" Olivia sat up as the words broke out. "She *liked* you! You're saying it was her? Jane Lawson was your first?"

Scott nodded, his expression stiff, but his eyes full of conflicted emotion.

"How old was she then?"

"I don't know. Late thirties."

"Late thirties? She was in her late thirties, and you were seventeen? And she had sex with you?"

Scott cleared his throat again. "It wasn't like you're making it sound. I wanted to. I was seventeen and still a virgin. Of course I wanted to."

"But the fact that you were a virgin makes it worse. She was totally in control. You worked for her. You were seventeen!" She was so outraged she was shaking with it. She'd seen Jane Lawson around town quite a bit growing up, although the woman had moved out west several years ago. There was no possible way she could hide her indignation, even though her response was obviously making Scott uncomfortable.

"I was old enough to make a decision about sex."

"Maybe you were. But that doesn't make it right. Did you... did you come on to her or something?"

"No. Of course not. I can't possibly overstate how clueless I was with women. I never would have done *anything*. She came on to me."

"Oh my God, Scott. Oh my God."

He sat up too, looking frustrated now as well as uncomfortable. "Stop making it sound so bad. She didn't force me. She didn't do anything even close to forcing me."

"I'm not saying she forced you. It doesn't have to be forced to still be... really wrong. Did it just happen once?"

He shook his head. "All summer."

"Oh my God, Scott."

"Stop saying that. It wasn't bad like you're making it sound. I... liked it. I learned a lot. I was happy to learn a lot. It was just..."

"Sex? Is that what you're going to say? It was just sex?" She was still shaking a little with the intensity of her feelings.

"It was. Just sex."

"You were a shy seventeen-year-old virgin, and she was your boss. She took advantage of you. You do see that, don't you? Just because you were a boy and not a girl doesn't make it all right."

"Sure, I see that. I get it. I learned later that she did it almost every summer—with a different guy, I mean. But I'm telling you that it wasn't traumatic for me."

"I believe you. It doesn't have to be traumatic to still be really wrong."

He stared at her, looking as breathless and emotional as she felt.

"And you're telling me that what happened—that it happened that way—didn't have any effect on you? You, who just told me he's slept with fifty-six women but none of them more than once or twice. Except her, I assume."

"Except her."

They were both sitting up on the bed, the covers down around their laps. She reached over to stroke his bristly jaw with her fingertips. "She used you, Scott. It wasn't right."

Something seemed to be shuddering inside him. Something that was making him shake just slightly but that he wouldn't let loose. He sat there, perfectly still, letting her stroke his face.

She felt it shuddering in her too.

"I know it wasn't right," he whispered at last. "I know."

"It doesn't have to be like that."

"What doesn't?"

"Sex. It doesn't have to be like that. It can be real. It can be... giving. Not taking."

"I know it can."

"But you've never really experienced it?"

"I've... tried."

She couldn't stand it. She simply couldn't stand it. The man who'd held her last night, who'd talked to her, who'd been so worried that he'd hurt her feelings, wasn't a man who should have tried fifty-six times to find something real in sex and never actually found it.

She couldn't let it remain that way.

She had to change it.

She had to fix it.

She wanted to more than she'd ever wanted anything.

She leaned forward to kiss him softly on the lips.

His mouth clung to hers, and his hand rose up to tangle in her hair. "Olivia," he breathed.

She felt him pulling back, so she waited until she heard him murmur, "Yes. Please." Then she moved forward, brushing her lips against his even more.

"Olivia, don't do this because you feel sorry for me," he murmured, his mouth still clinging to hers.

"I'm not. I don't feel sorry for you. I want to do this."

"Really?"

"Yes. Really. More than anything." She did withdraw then, enough to look him in the eyes. "Don't you?"

Something burst into life in his eyes. She saw it happen. He took her head in both his hands. "Yes," he said thickly, just before he kissed her again. "I do."

8

As Scott was kissing Olivia, both of them sitting up in the bed, he was briefly afraid that his heart would beat its way out of his chest.

For a moment he believed it might actually happen.

He'd never felt like this before—not once in his life. Like a presence in his chest had burst open, exploded, and was getting bigger as the seconds passed. Like it would soon be too big to fit inside him.

And if that wasn't enough, he'd grown aroused so quickly it almost hurt, his erection tight in his underwear and aching so deeply it would have overwhelmed him had he not been feeling so many other things at the same time.

He had no time or space to think it through or settle his emotions or even take a full breath. The only thing he was capable of doing was kissing Olivia as much as he could.

His fingers were tangled in her loose hair, and he was

holding her head still so he could press his lips harder against hers. Her tongue was deep in his mouth, doing such delicious things he couldn't begin to sort through specific moves.

After a minute, she put her hands on his chest and pushed him backward onto the bed, moving on top of him so she could keep kissing him as he reclined. Then she was all over him, her legs straddling his hips, her breasts brushing against his chest, her hair spilling down over both of them.

Before he realized what was happening, she was pulling his T-shirt up over his head. He had to release her to let her pull it off his arms, and he moaned helplessly as she kissed her way down his neck, his collarbone, and lower to take his nipple in her mouth.

He rocked his pelvis up against the weight of her, his erection getting aching, exquisite relief from the pressure. She whimpered and ground down in response. His neck arched up, and he released an embarrassing groan of pleasure.

This was Olivia Holiday. On top of him in bed. And she was making him feel so good.

She wanted him.

No fantasy he'd ever had could possibly equal this.

"Scott," she murmured, still mouthing her way across his chest. "Did I lose you somewhere?"

"No! God, no." He pushed his chest up into her mouth when she flicked his other nipple with her tongue. "I'm here. I'm here all the way."

"Good. I like you here." She rubbed her whole body against him, and he took her bottom in his hands, holding the soft, firm flesh through the stretched fabric of her leggings.

She lifted her head and smiled down on him, flushed and breathless.

She was on fire. All her inner shining breaking out in blinding flames.

For him.

Him.

He pulled her down into another deep kiss and didn't stop kissing her until she pulled away again.

This time she kissed her way down past his nipples. To his belly. And even lower.

"Oh fuck, Olivia, you don't have to do that." She was pulling down his underwear, and it felt like his erection was straining toward her hands.

"I want to."

"But I wanted to do you." He sounded foolish, like a boy. But it was true. He wanted to please her. Please her as much as he was capable of.

"Well, I'm doing you first. Then you can do me if you want. Then maybe we can do some things together." She was still smiling, still shining for him. The strap of her tank top had slipped off one of her shoulders, and he wanted to bite the gorgeous, graceful curve of bare skin displayed there.

When he didn't answer, she paused. "Is that all right?"

He gave a breathless laugh as she pulled his boxer briefs off his feet. "That's pretty okay with me."

"Good." She was still beaming as she kissed a line from his belly button down toward his groin.

He held his breath when she neared his erection, which was thick and hard and folded up toward his stomach.

She stared down at him for a minute before she took it in both her hands, holding it almost gently.

He bucked up slightly at the light touch of her fingers and then bucked up again when she stroked him purposefully.

He was going to embarrass himself. He knew it. He had almost no control at the moment, and every little thing she did was pushing him further toward the edge.

"Fuck," he heard himself mutter. "Oh fuck, Olivia."

"I haven't even done anything yet." She was changing positions, lowering her face toward his groin.

She'd touched him, and that had been more than enough.

He knew what was coming as she eyed her fingers around his shaft, and he tried to prepare himself for it.

But nothing could prepare him for the feel of her mouth all around him. His hips arched up off the bed, and he tightened his fists in her hair, using every restraint he had left not to pull her hair too hard.

She sucked him a couple of times before she let him slip from her mouth. It sounded like she was smiling some more as she murmured, "I guess that means you like it."

"Like it? *Like* it? Oh fuck, you're going to kill me before the end of this."

She held his erection upright so she could lick a line up the length of it. Then she teased the head with her tongue until he was moaning loudly and tossing his head like a teenage boy getting lucky for the first time.

When she cupped and squeezed his balls, he almost lost it. His whole body throbbed dangerously and then kept throbbing when she wrapped her mouth around him again. She established a steady rhythm at last, and he couldn't help but thrust into it, making sure he wasn't too rough since she obviously didn't want him to fuck her throat.

"Oh fuck, that's so good." He was muttering again. He couldn't hold back the words. "Oh fuck, just like that. Just like that. Fuck, you feel so good. You're making me feel so good."

She murmured wordless encouragement and sped up her rhythm, squeezing his balls again in a way that whited out his vision momentarily.

He reached up to grab for the headboard as pleasure sliced through him. "Shit, I'm close, Olivia. I'm gonna... gonna... gonna..."

Then it didn't matter what he was saying because he was coming long and hard, releasing loud, naked moans as she sucked him through the spasms.

Climax took him so powerfully that he was utterly leveled when the waves of pleasure finally faded. He collapsed onto the bed, one arm stretched out on the bed and the other still curved around Olivia's head.

She was smiling as she let him slip out of her mouth and straightened up. "That was pretty good, wasn't it?"

He grunted. It was all he could manage.

She giggled and stretched out on top of him, kissing him slow and sweet as she pressed the full length of her body against him. "I thought it was pretty good too."

She seemed to mean it. As if pleasing him had genuinely pleased her.

He wasn't going to leave it at that though. As soon as he could catch his breath and make himself move, he was going to make her feel just as good as she'd made him.

It took a few minutes, but eventually he was able to start stroking Olivia's body. She was still sprawled on top of him, and her warm weight was so sexy. He slid his hands up and down from her hair to her back to her ass to her thighs, and he couldn't get his fill of the shape, the texture of her.

She pressed a few kisses into his neck and shifted on top of him as he caressed her more intentionally. Then he found the focus to turn her over onto her back and move over her. He kissed her again, his hand lingering on the soft, delicious place where her butt met the back of her thighs. Then he straightened up so he could pull off her tank top and finally see her bare breasts.

He stared hotly, so long that she must have gotten self-conscious. "Aren't you going to do anything but look?" she asked.

"Yes. I'm going to do a lot more than look." His voice was too thick, but there was no help for that. He lowered his head and flicked one of her rosy nipples with his tongue.

Her breath hitched, so he did it again. Then he took more of her breast into his mouth and suckled as skillfully as he could.

"Oh God, Scott," she mumbled, arching her neck the way he had earlier. "That's a lot better than looking."

He chuckled around her breast and worked on pleasing her as much as he could. It didn't take long before she was whimpering helplessly and trying to grind her arousal against his hip.

She was really turned on. She wasn't trying to hide it. She wrapped one of her legs around him and squeezed until he huffed.

He was already getting hard again, but he wasn't going to let that distract him. Nothing mattered as much as giving her as much pleasure as she'd given him.

Pretty soon she was begging him softly to make her come and rocking her hips up into him. When her pleas turned desperate, he lifted his head and slowly pulled down her leggings. The little underwear she wore came with them so she was completely naked when he'd taken them off.

"You're the most beautiful woman I've ever seen," he said.

"Don't exaggerate." Her cheeks were very pink now and her eyes heavy with desire.

"I'm not exaggerating. You're the most beautiful woman in the world. I've always thought so."

He couldn't believe he was telling her that, but he couldn't seem to hold anything back from her right now. All of it was coming out.

Her face tightened briefly, as if his words meant something to her. Then she pulled him down into a kiss. He responded immediately, but he could feel she was really turned on by her whimpering and writhing, so after a minute he pulled away and kissed his way back down her body.

When he had one of her breasts in his mouth, he moved one hand between her legs, opening her up with his fingers, feeling how hot and wet she was.

She wanted this so much.

She wanted him.

"Scott, please. Oh please."

He slid one finger inside her and then two, curling them up so he could stroke her inner walls. She arched up dramatically and tried to ride his fingers as he kept suckling her breast.

He knew she was close, but he was surprised by how quickly she came, her body tightening all around his fingers as her hips rode out her release.

She was making the most delicious sounds of pleasure, and he hadn't had nearly enough of them, so he kept his fingers inside her and lowered his mouth even more until he could lick her clit.

She thrust her hips up with a little sob, squeezing around him deliciously, so he licked her again.

"Scott, oh God, Scott! I'm going to come again."

He knew she would. She kept clenching around his fingers and shamelessly rocking her hips. He had to fight to keep her still enough for him to keep his mouth on her clit.

She was clutching at the headboard with both hands and sobbing out her pleasure as she came and then came again.

It was intoxicating and more than that. Strangely emotional. That he was doing this for her. That she wanted him to. That he was allowed to.

When she came a fourth time, he heard her babbling out, "Enough," so he raised his head and gently slid his fingers out. They were soaked with her arousal, and he couldn't resist sliding the fingers into his mouth so he could suck them clean. He was as hard as rock again, but his body wasn't the only part of him blown away by what was happening here.

She was watching him with hot, heavy eyes. "Thank you."

"I enjoyed it as much as you did."

"Maybe not quite as much."

"I bet I did."

She gestured for him, and he came to her so they could kiss again. This time he slowed it down so he could take his time, letting her recover as they kissed without pushing them into more before she was ready.

Eventually her hand stroked down his back, squeezed his ass, and then moved around his body until she was feeling the hard length of him. "I guess this means you're interested in more," she said in a teasing voice.

"Only if you are."

"I definitely am. I haven't even felt you inside me yet." She pushed him over onto his back, but before she moved on top of him, she paused. "We need a condom."

"Shit." It hadn't even occurred to him. That was how far gone he was.

"I've got one in my purse. Don't move."

He was so turned on again that he wasn't sure he was capable of moving at the moment, so he was relieved that she ran into the other room to her purse and then ran back in less than thirty seconds.

She had a condom packet in her hand when she climbed back onto the bed, and she was grinning as she ripped it open and rolled it on over the length of him.

Then she was straddling his hips again. His lips parted as he watched in heated awe as she lined herself up over him and then sheathed him with her body.

Both of them groaned at the penetration, and he reached out so he could hold on to her hips to keep her in place.

She started to move slowly, just rocking over him as if she were trying out the position, figuring out what worked the best.

"Is this good for you?" she asked after a minute.

"God, yes. Just being inside you is good for me." He was

speaking the absolute truth. Nothing—not anything he'd ever done—had been better than this.

She smiled as if she'd liked that he'd said that. Gradually she intensified her rhythm and her motion over him until she was riding him hard. He gripped the soft flesh of her ass and thrust up into her. Both of them were grunting loudly now, and he knew she was going to come soon. He just hoped she did before he lost control.

She was moving so vigorously now that her breasts bounced erotically. She was giving him everything. She wasn't putting on a pose or pretense or trying to act the way he wanted. This was real. All her. She was with him fully. All the way.

She cried out loudly as she reached climax, gasping about how good it was, how hard she was coming. He almost came with her as her channel clamped down around him, and he let out an embarrassingly uncontrolled shout as he tried to hold himself back.

He just barely did it, still hard and urgent as he turned them over so she was on her back and he was between her thighs.

"Can you wrap your legs around me?" he rasped. "I want to feel you all around me."

She did as he asked, hooking her ankles to keep them secure. "Like this?"

"Yeah. Just like that."

"You're going to come this time, aren't you?"

He was pretty sure he wasn't going to be able to help it. "You want me to?"

"Oh yeah. I want us to do this together."

He kissed her gently. "We are together."

He never would have believed it, even yesterday morning, but they were together in this. He knew it for sure.

"Yeah," she breathed, tightening her thighs in a way that made him jerk his hips. "We're together."

He started to thrust then, fast and steady and no holding back. She was moving with him, and together they were shaking the bed, making matching sounds of effort and pleasure. His eyes were blurring over now, and sweat was dripping down his face. And Olivia was everything.

The entire rotation of the planet was centered in her.

"Scott," Olivia gasped, as her motion grew more clumsy, urgent.

"Olivia."

"Scott, this is us. All of us." She was tightening around him again, and her face was twisting in pleasure.

"Yeah."

"You and me. This is all of us."

He understood what she was saying, what she was giving him. She was sharing herself—her body, her heart, her humanity, all her bright shining—and she was recognizing, appreciating, wanting all his humanity too.

"Yes. Olivia." He couldn't say anything else. Just her name in a breathless huff as he fell over the edge.

His hips jerked helplessly as he fell out of rhythm, but she was right there with him as the waves of sensation overwhelmed him. Both of them were shouting with it, riding it out until they'd taken and given all they could.

If he'd been leveled after his earlier climax, he was more than that now. He fell down on top of her, his elbows buckling completely. She huffed when his weight landed on her, and he tried to ease some of it off. But he could barely move. Couldn't do more than press a few clumsy kisses into her neck.

She was stroking his back and his head, and he loved the feel of it.

It felt... tender.

And he wasn't sure anyone had ever really been tender with him before.

But he could feel his erection softening, and the condom was going to be a problem. So before he'd fully recovered, before he wanted to, he had to pull himself out and take care of it.

It was messy and strangely difficult to manage, and he swayed on his feet when he tried to stand up.

"You okay?" she asked softly from the bed.

"Yeah."

"You want me to get that?"

"Nah. I got it."

He wasn't sure he really had it, but the condom was in his hand, so he tied it off and limped to the bathroom to throw it away.

It was dark in there, and he'd forgotten the flashlight, so he had to leave the door cracked as he washed his hands and then cleaned himself off. He stood in front of the sink and tried to catch his breath, but he couldn't.

He was wiped out. In more ways than one.

It didn't feel safe.

He wasn't sure he was equipped to handle this.

It had been years since he'd ever felt so weak.

He splashed water onto his face in an attempt to revive himself, but it didn't work. His face still wet, he bent at the waist and gasped a few times, holding on to the vanity for support.

What the hell was wrong with him?

"Hey." Olivia's soft voice. From right outside the bathroom door. "Are you okay?"

He straightened up so quickly it hurt. "Yeah. Yeah." He reached for a hand towel to dry his face.

"Are you sure?" She was coming into the bathroom now. She'd brought the flashlight and flipped it on.

He'd rather it be dark so she wouldn't be able to see him clearly. "Yeah. Of course." He tried very hard to make his voice sound natural.

He'd never expected to have sex with Olivia, and it was some sort of miracle that it had been good for both of them.

But he'd be damned if he let her see that it affected him so much he was about to have a breakdown now that it was over.

She wrapped an arm around his waist and pressed a kiss against his shoulder. "Scott? Talk to me. You're shaking. What's the matter?"

Shit. He didn't do this. He wasn't going to do this. He wasn't that teenage boy anymore. "I said it was nothing. I think I might have overexerted myself earlier."

Surely that would be convincing.

Olivia wasn't convinced. She was frowning in concern. "Scott?" She tightened an arm around him, and he wanted her comfort, her support so much he had to pull away.

He saw her surprise on her face. Then he saw a flicker of hurt that followed it.

"Sorry," he said quickly, gruffly. "Sorry. I just need a little... space."

She was silent for a tense moment, and he knew he'd made a mistake.

But he didn't know what else he could do unless he was prepared to completely fall apart right here in the bathroom.

In front of Olivia.

Because of Olivia.

"Sure," she said, her expression changing, her mouth turning up into a smile. "No problem. I get it."

There was something fake about her smile and her casual tone that pierced him through the heart. "I'm sorry, Oliv—"

"Don't be sorry," she said with another smile, her tone a bit more convincing this time. "We both had a really good time, didn't we?"

"Y-yeah."

"I think we both needed it. It doesn't have to be any more than that. You can have all the space you want."

He opened his mouth, trying to make this better, trying to get her back. It felt like she'd retreated forever out of his reach.

But no words came out.

She shook her head with another smile. "But would you mind if I have my space in the bathroom. I need to pee again."

"Oh. Yeah. Of course."

He stepped out, and she closed the door in his face.

He didn't move. Not for a long time. Not until he heard the toilet flush.

He'd blown it. Completely.

He'd always been clueless with women, and he wasn't sure why ten years of trying to be a different man would ever really change that.

9

Olivia cried a little bit in the bathroom but just for a minute and so softly that there would be no way for Scott to hear.

She didn't like to be stupid.

She usually didn't think she was.

But she might have been a bit stupid here with Scott.

She'd been hoping it was more than sex.

She'd been hoping it might last beyond this weird, intense snow-surrounded world they'd been living in for the past twenty hours.

But his asking for space the way he had couldn't be good. Only a fool would think that didn't mean something. She cringed as she remembered how sappily she'd come into the bathroom to comfort him when it looked like he was hurting.

Maybe he had been hurting, but he didn't want comfort from her.

He'd wanted sex and companionship for the night, and that was what he'd gotten.

She'd gotten it too, so she shouldn't complain.

She was a grown-up. Smart and realistic no matter what everyone thought of her. She wasn't going to be silly about this.

So she was calm and in control of her emotions as she came out of the bathroom, wearing the same white robe she'd put on yesterday.

She found Scott in the living room making a fire. He'd put on his jeans and T-shirt, and his hair was standing up on end.

Making sure she sounded light and easy, she said, "There's cereal, and the milk might still be okay since it's been so cold in here, so we at least have something for breakfast."

He was poking at the small flame he'd just got going, and he didn't turn to look at her. "That's good."

She watched him for a moment—his stiff shoulders, his impassive face.

He wasn't the boy from long ago, and he wasn't the confident, careless man he'd been for the past ten years.

She wasn't sure who he was, except he had a wall around his expression that might never come down.

It was fine.

She wasn't a fool.

One night of sex didn't mean anything. It didn't mean he wanted to share his life with her the way it had felt they'd been sharing themselves since they'd arrived here yesterday.

Her cheeks burned as she remembered how vulnerable she'd made herself, all the utterly naked things she'd said in his arms less than an hour ago.

No wonder he'd pulled away afterward.

Any guy would have.

Girls weren't supposed to go all in like that the first time they had sex with a guy.

Mortified and still more crushed than she'd ever admit to a living soul, she walked into the kitchen to get out the milk, cereal, juice, and two bowls. The milk was just fine. It didn't feel any warmer than it normally would have been, and it smelled fresh.

After a minute, Scott came to join her, and they ate a quiet breakfast on the stools at the small kitchen island.

She caught him eyeing her a couple of times, but he didn't let his gaze linger. Neither did she.

He finished his cereal, put his spoon down, and said, "Olivia."

Her gaze jumped to his strained face. The dark stubble on his jaw made him look sexy, almost dangerous, and the unmistakable Matheson eyes were deep and striking. She waited for him to continue.

"I'm sorry."

It hurt. So much she had to hide a wince from the pain in her heart. "You don't have to be sorry," she said with as bright a smile as she could manage. "I get it. I really do."

His brows drew together. "You do?"

"Yeah. Last night was great. Like I said before, both of us needed it. But you're not worried I'm thinking it's more than that, are you? Because you and me together—outside this cottage—it just doesn't make any sense, does it? So if you're worried I'm wanting more than last night, then you really don't have to. I don't."

"You don't?"

"I don't. I promise."

He stared at her fixedly. For far too long. "Okay."

"Okay?"

"Yes. Okay. We're... good then."

"Yes. We're good. So we can stop being weird with each other and get back to normal." She didn't feel normal. She felt like her face might crack from the attempt to keep her expression in place. But she was doing this, and it was going to be convincing.

Scott was never going to know how stupid she'd been with him.

No one was ever going to know.

"Okay. Back to normal then." He cleared his throat and stood up. He looked out through the big window at the front of the cottage and then back to her.

His face contorted strangely for a moment before the expression was gone.

"Scott?" she asked, confused by what she'd seen in his face.

He opened his mouth to say something, but just then

there was a popping sound and all the lights came on. The heat pump kicked on, and the refrigerator started to buzz.

"Well, that's good," she said, hardly recognizing the room around her after seeing everything with nothing but firelight for so long.

"Yeah." He stretched his arms one by one and looked outside. "I'm going to shovel out the front walk so we can get outside."

"Okay. Good idea. There's a shovel in the storage room."

He put on his sweater, coat, socks, and shoes and then went outside. Olivia stood where she was and watched him through the window for a while, feeling heavy. Kind of sick.

When she heard a phone ringing in the room, it took a minute to figure out what the sound even was. It had felt for so long like she and Scott were alone in the world, but they weren't.

They weren't.

She found her phone and answered it when she saw it was her sister Rebecca.

"Hey, are you all right?" Rebecca asked when Olivia greeted her.

"Yeah. I'm fine. Ready for this ordeal to be over."

"Was it terrible?"

"N-no. It wasn't terrible. How are you and Phil?"

"We're fine. We made it to Richmond before the snow. Are you sure you're okay, Olivia? You sound upset."

"I do not sound upset."

"Please. We shared a room until I was ten. I know what your 'I'm really upset but trying to pretend I'm not' voice sounds like. What's going on?"

Olivia swallowed over a painful lump in her throat. "It's nothing really. It's... Scott."

"Did something happen?"

"Yeah. It did."

Rebecca was silent for a moment. "I always knew you were into him. Why else would you have it out for him the way you did?"

"I'm not into him. I mean, I wasn't. I don't think I was."

"But you are now?"

"It doesn't matter. He's not into me."

"He might be. Who can possibly know what's going on beneath that I'm-king-of-the-world act he puts on?"

Olivia knew what was going on beneath his act.

At least she'd thought she did.

"He's not, Rebecca. I thought we had... a really good night, and it felt like we were... sharing stuff that was pretty deep. But the first thing he told me afterward was that he needs space."

"You're kidding. That's kind of cold."

"I thought so." A tear was beading on her eyelashes, so she quickly wiped it away.

"I'm really sorry, Olivia. I know that's got to hurt."

"It's okay. I'm really not stupid about things, you know."

"I know you're not stupid. But it's not stupid to hope for something with a guy if you thought there was reason."

"I thought there was. But I was wrong. And I'm not going to whine about it or hold on to something that's never going to happen."

"Maybe he meant what he said. About needing space. Maybe he really does need some."

"Well, I'm giving it to him!"

"I know that. I just mean maybe he wasn't trying to blow you off. You said you shared a lot of deep stuff? He doesn't do that. I don't know him very well, but I'd bet he never does that. Maybe it was hard for him. Really hard. Maybe he just needs a little time to wrap his head around what's happening before he moves forward."

Olivia felt herself leaning into the words, clinging to them, hoping desperately that they were right. But she caught herself almost immediately. "No. You always think the best in everyone, but usually people don't lead with their best. I'm not going to concoct some sort of ridiculous fantasy about what happened. We had sex. Then he pulled back, pushed me away. Any fool knows what that means."

"Maybe. Maybe not."

"Rebecca, please don't encourage me to be stupid."

"You're not stupid, Olivia. I know Dad made you think you were, but you were never stupid. And you know, one thing I've learned since this summer is that sometimes love isn't smart. It can't be smart. It's better than smart. It takes everything."

Olivia was shaking, her eyes blurring over. "I don't love Scott."

"Okay."

"I don't."

"I said okay."

"And he doesn't want... everything from me."

"I'm sorry."

Olivia took a couple of deep breaths and got control of her trembling. "Thanks, Rebecca."

"You're welcome."

"I'm hoping Ed and Chuck will dig us out of this by the afternoon. The power came back on, so at least we're not in the dark anymore."

"Let me know how it goes."

Olivia felt a little better when she hung up, and she went to the window and looked out.

Scott was shoveling fast and hard. He'd already cleared the walk from the storage room to the front door and half the walk down to the driveway.

She watched his strong, lean body in his heavy coat and wondered if Rebecca was right about him.

Opening up last night had been hard for him. Olivia knew it had. Maybe he was genuinely trying to figure out how he felt and he wasn't just trying to get away from her.

It didn't mean there was hope for them, but it would make her feel better. Like she hadn't made up what happened between them because she wanted it so much.

As she was staring at him, he straightened up and turned to face her, as if he'd sensed her presence. They gazed at each other through the window in silence, neither of them moving.

His expression was sober, almost aching. No trace of his characteristic amused irony.

She didn't know what he was seeing on her face, but he wasn't turning away from it.

Their shared gaze lasted longer than it should, and she couldn't drag herself away until her phone rang again.

This time it was Ed, telling her that they'd finished plowing the parking lots at Holiday Acres and were starting on the roads.

In a few hours, Olivia and Scott would be able to leave this cottage at last.

It was two o'clock in the afternoon when she and Scott parked his SUV in a parking spot near the farmhouse. The private roads were clear enough to drive, and when Chuck had reached the driveway to Mistletoe Cottage, he'd helped Scott push his car out of the ditch.

Now Olivia was home, and Scott hadn't said a word the entire drive back.

"Okay," she said when he put the SUV into park. "Thanks."

"For what?"

"For driving me back. For... everything."

He turned his head to meet her eyes. "You're welcome. Thank you."

She nodded and took a quick breath. "Are we... are we okay with everything?"

"Yes. As long as you're okay."

"I guess I am. It feels... awkward. If you want to..." She shook her head, wondering what the hell she was even trying to say.

"If I want to what?"

"I don't know. I guess it's just one of those things." She remembered what Rebecca had said and made herself be brave. "But it meant a lot to me. Last night did. It meant a lot."

"It meant a lot to me too." Scott's hands were clenched around the steering wheel, and his voice was thicker than normal.

She waited to see if he'd say anything else, but he didn't. She nodded again and unbuckled her seat belt. "I'll see you around, Scott."

"See you around."

And that was it. Whatever had happened between them was evidently over.

She got out of his car and closed the door behind her.

The county roads weren't all clear yet, so it might be iffy for him to try to get home. He should be getting out of his car so he could hang out in the store or the coffee shop until the roads were clearer.

But he didn't. And he didn't back out of his parking space and drive away.

He stayed in the driver's seat of his car as she walked

carefully up the still slippery sidewalk that led to the front door of the old farmhouse.

She glanced back once, but Scott still hadn't moved.

She wanted to go back to him.

She *needed* to go back to him.

But she didn't.

10

SCOTT COULDN'T MOVE.

He was paralyzed, trapped in place, holding on to the steering wheel like it was the only way to hold himself together.

He wasn't sure how long he sat there. He was stuck in an emotional daze so all-consuming that he was taken completely by surprise when the door of his SUV suddenly opened and someone climbed in to sit in the passenger seat.

He jerked in shock and focused on the intruder.

Not Olivia.

Russ. His uncle. Sitting there looking at him like it was perfectly normal for him to have gotten into the car uninvited.

"What's going on here?" Russ asked. He had the Matheson eyes and brown hair about the same shade as Scott's, but his had a sprinkling of gray in it. He'd been eighteen when Scott was born.

"What do you mean?"

"I mean you've been sitting here for ten minutes, and I'm not blind. Something is wrong."

"It's not important."

"Really?"

"Yes, really."

"Then why do you look like the slightest impact would shatter you into pieces?"

Because it would. Scott was genuinely afraid that it would.

"Hey. Scott. Talk to me." Russ had turned in the passenger seat to face him.

"There's nothing to talk about."

"Damn it," Russ muttered. "You boys are all the same. All three of you."

Scott was surprised by the vehemence and couldn't think of a response.

"You know, I loved your father. He was a lot older than me, so we were never very close, but he was my brother and I loved him. He had it much harder than I did growing up since our folks didn't have any extra money until I was born. He had to work really hard. A lot harder than me." Russ sighed and leaned his head back against the seat. "He didn't get a chance to go to college. He didn't have a lot of the things I had as a boy. He had it rough."

Scott's eyebrows had arched as he listened. Russ wasn't

prone to rambling about anything—certainly not personal history. "I know he did. He let us know it all the time."

"I know. He had it rough, and it took its toll on him. And then he took that toll out on you boys. I wasn't around, so I didn't see it, but I can see the aftermath."

"What aftermath?"

"What happened because he didn't know how to love you boys and because your mama died too soon." Russ shook his head. "He didn't teach you how to love. He taught Kent to hide and Phil to run away and you to..."

"To what?" Scott was deeply torn but also becoming defensive. "He taught me to what?"

"To put on a mask for the world. To never be vulnerable. To always try to be someone you aren't."

Scott had always liked Russ, and they'd gotten along well for the past four years, ever since Russ had moved back home from Richmond. But he'd never realized Russ knew him as well, as deeply, as this. "I don't always do that."

"Yes, you do. You know you do. You haven't been yourself since you went to college."

Scott tried to object, but he couldn't bring himself to lie to his uncle like that, not when Russ was being so open with him. "It wasn't just Dad."

Russ blinked. "What else was it?"

Scott didn't answer.

"Did something else happen?"

Of course it had happened. Life happened. And life

tore you apart without fail and only occasionally put you together again.

"Scott? Is there something you need to tell me?"

His uncle was normally sardonic, distantly amused. It was unnerving to see him like this. "No," Scott said hoarsely. "Nothing. Just life."

He'd told Olivia. He wasn't sure he'd ever tell anyone else about how he'd lost his virginity, how he'd learned to understand the nature of sex until Olivia had taught him it could be something else.

"So now that you know what you're doing, you should be able to take the mask off. Right?"

Scott stared at his uncle blankly.

"Olivia deserves better from you. She deserves the real thing."

For no good reason, Scott was hit with a wave of anger. He lashed out. "Fuck you, Russ. Who are you to tell me what Olivia deserves? When have you ever even tried for the real thing? You sit there and watch the world go by from a safe distance. You've never even tried to be in love. Who are you to lecture me about it?"

Russ winced slightly, like he'd been hit. But his voice was mild when he replied, "You're right. Maybe I'm a hypocrite. Maybe I have no ground to stand on when it comes to this. But you're wrong about my never being in love. And at least I tried to step up."

"What? You did?" Scott was as astonished at this as he would have been if Russ had told him he'd sprouted wings and flown.

"Yeah. I did. I tried, and it didn't work. And maybe that's her final answer and I'll have to live with it, but at least I gave it a try. Did you try? Did you really try to step up?"

Scott's vision blurred, the question hitting him hard.

"Maybe being a Matheson means we have these weird brown eyes and we're all emotionally damaged. Family can do that to you. But Phil stepped up, and he's happy now. He's getting better. Why the hell shouldn't the same be true of you?"

"Rebecca loves Phil. Olivia doesn't—"

"Do you know that? For sure? Did you even give her the option?"

No. He hadn't. He'd pulled away like a wounded animal who was terrified of getting hurt again, who had to show the world only teeth and claws because its underbelly was too soft.

Russ went on. "The Holidays might have had it better than you did growing up. At least they had a mother who loved them. But they didn't have an easy father either, and they had to learn to be strong and rely on themselves, rather than trusting in men to take care of them. That means they're never going to make it easy. They're not going to let down their guard unless they know for sure the man is offering them everything. That's true of Olivia as much as it is of the rest of them."

"Olivia doesn't want..." Scott trailed off, so rattled he couldn't finish the sentence.

"Then why was she crying just now as she came into the house?"

"She was crying?"

"Yes. I have to assume it was your doing. You might think about that for a minute."

Before Scott could form an answer, Russ was opening the passenger door and getting out. He said before he slammed it closed, "Your father didn't do right by you, but you can do right by her."

Scott was paralyzed again as he watched Russ take the few steps to the sidewalk. When his uncle stopped, looking out at the road, Scott turned to see what had distracted him.

It was Laura, driving slowly into the parking lot in one of the Holidays' SUVs. Before she'd barely put it in park, a small boy was jumping out of the car and running toward Russ.

Tommy. Laura's smart, fearless, brown-eyed son.

He slipped once as he ran, but he popped right back up, still grinning. When he reached Russ, he hurled himself at him in a hug.

The few times Scott had seen Russ interact with the boy, Russ had been amused and distant and ironic, which Tommy seemed to take as a game. But something had evidently changed because Russ lifted the boy up in a big hug.

Scott stared at them—his uncle and the six-year-old boy. Tommy obviously adored Russ, and there was something almost needy in Russ's embrace.

Without thinking, Scott turned to look at Laura, who had gotten out of the car too and was standing beside it, watching Russ hug her son. Laura was brown-haired like Olivia and about the same height, but she had freckles and a slimmer figure. She didn't shine like Olivia did, and she wasn't smiling even a little bit now.

After a minute, she turned and started to walk toward the house.

And that was when Scott remembered that Russ said Olivia had been crying.

And maybe he was the one who had made her cry.

Scott jumped out of the car and hurried after Laura, moving as fast as he could on the slick sidewalk.

Laura turned around when he caught up with her at the front door. "What do you want?"

"I need to talk to Olivia."

"I don't know where she is."

"She came in here. I assume she went to her room."

"Well, if she went to her room, I assume she wants to be alone." Laura was never soft, but she seemed sharper than normal, almost brittle, but Scott was too distracted to figure out why.

"I need to talk to her. I *need* to."

Laura rolled her eyes. "Well, you can come up and knock on her door, but if she doesn't let you in, you'll have to leave."

"Fine. I'll leave."

Scott walked up the stairs to the Holidays' private residence, and he tried not to shake with impatience as Laura didn't move as quickly as he wanted her to.

When they got into the main room, Laura gestured him down the hall. "Second room on the right."

He strode down the hall and knocked loudly on the door.

"I'm not in the mood for talking," Olivia called out from inside.

"Olivia?"

"Scott?" Her voice had changed, gotten slightly shrill. "What are you doing here? Go away!"

"I'm not going to go away. I want to talk. Let me in." He kept his voice as low as he could because if Laura heard his words, she was going to make him leave.

"We have nothing to talk about. I'm tired and want to be alone."

"You can be alone after we talk. Let me in."

Scott waited, breathless and shuddering with that deepening force in his chest that felt like it might burst open at any moment the way it had last night and again this morning.

Olivia swung open the door and glared at him across the threshold. Her hair was still loose and kinky from the way it had dried overnight, but she'd changed into a pair of loose cotton pajama pants in a white-and-black paisley pattern and a black T-shirt. "What's the matter with you, Scott? This is my bedroom."

"I know it's your bedroom, but you're in it. That's why I'm here."

She made a frustrated gust of sound. "What do you want?"

"I told you. I wanted to talk." He glanced down the hall when he saw motion. Laura, walking to where she could see him, evidently to see if she needed to make him leave or not. "Please," he added hoarsely, turning back to Olivia.

She made an impatient face. "Fine. Come in."

He stepped into the room and shut the door behind him. He tried not to look at the rumpled double bed, which she'd clearly been lying in just now.

Searching her face, he thought he might see a trace of tears, but mostly she looked annoyed with him.

Not just annoyed.

Angry.

She was angry with him.

He frowned. "Are you mad at me?"

"No, I'm not mad."

"You look mad."

"I just said I wasn't mad!"

"And I'm saying you look mad. You look like you want to bite my head off."

"I do want to bite your head off," she snapped.

He blinked. "Why? You said everything was okay."

"Well, I lied," she burst out. "I lied! It's not okay. It sucks. It's terrible! And I don't care if I should be smart enough to know that having sex once doesn't mean it's anything real, but it felt real to me, and then you said you needed space. Space! I was giving you space, and now here you are pounding on my bedroom door looking like... you."

That pressure inside his chest had exploded and then exploded again. "I am me."

"I mean the real you. The *real* you. You look like..." She shook her head fiercely. "So screw you, Scott Matheson. You don't get to jerk me around like this. If you want to be that invulnerable jackass, then you go right ahead and be him. You just better keep him away from me. You don't get to be with me unless it's really you."

She was fierce. Shining. Blazing with passion and feeling and sincerity.

And Scott didn't care if she was telling him off right now. She was everything he'd always wanted, and she was standing less than a foot away.

There was no way he could resist the compulsion. He reached out. Took her face in his hands. Kissed her hard.

"It's really me," he murmured against her lips. "Olivia, it's really me."

11

OLIVIA HAD NO IDEA WHAT WAS HAPPENING, BUT THERE WAS no way she could stop herself from kissing Scott back.

She'd crawled in bed as soon as she'd gotten in her room, hiding under the covers and trying to convince herself her heart wasn't broken.

It was harder than it should have been.

Then he'd pounded on her door and demanded to come in, and she'd lost it in more ways than one.

So now she was kissing him, letting him push her back against the wall and slide his tongue into her mouth. He was hard. Urgent. Hot as fire. Nothing at all like the nonchalant charmer he'd pretended to be for so long.

He'd said this was him. Really him.

And she believed him.

This was who she wanted. Not the face he'd been showing to the world.

His hands were moving over her body, sliding down to

cup her bottom over her pajama pants. She lifted one of her legs to wrap it around his thighs, trying to get even closer to him, trying to feel him as much as she could.

"Olivia," he said, tearing his mouth away and lowering his head to nuzzle her neck.

"Hmm?" She arched against the wall when she felt one of his hands sliding against the seam in her pants, right over where she was hottest.

"Is it really me you want?"

Maybe in a different context the question would have been confusing, but she knew exactly what he was asking.

He needed her to want the real him, the deepest part of him. Not just the hot man with a cocky attitude.

"Are you blind?" Her hands were fisted in his thick hair, holding his head in place since his tongue was doing miraculous things to the pulse point in her throat. "I've never wanted anyone the way I want you. The real you."

He made a guttural sound and nipped the skin of her neck, causing her to cry out and arch against the wall. She almost lost her balance since one of her legs was still wrapped around him, but he caught her before her knee buckled.

Giggling, they clung to each other for a minute, and the embrace turned into a tight hug that felt needy, naked, incredibly emotional.

Then Scott scooped her up and carried her over to the bed, toeing off his shoes and then moving over her as he laid her down. She pulled him fully on top of her, spreading her legs to make room for his body, and she was smiling like a fool as he kissed her again.

Scott desperately needed to shave. His bristles scratched up her face as he devoured her mouth. But she loved the feel of it. And the feel of the heat from his body pressing into hers. The texture of his jeans through the thin fabric of her pants. The hard bulge she could already feel at his groin.

Everything about him was tense and rough and deep and hard. And she loved it.

"Olivia," he mumbled, pressing sweet little kisses at the corners of her mouth, on her cheeks. "I'm sorry I said I needed space. I was... overwhelmed. And scared shitless. I don't want space from you."

She was so happy it felt like it was spilling out of her as she wrapped both her legs around him. "Good. Because you're not getting any space anytime soon."

He was smiling too as he gazed down on her.

She rubbed herself against the bulge of his erection, and she giggled when he winced.

"You shouldn't enjoy taunting me so much," he said thickly.

"I'm just trying to encourage you to hurry up. I'm not taunting you."

He leaned down until he was just a whisper away from kissing her again. "Everything about you taunts me. It always has."

"If that's true, then now that you can have me, why are you taking so long?"

"Just enjoying it. Trying to wrap my head around a world where this is actually happening."

"Well, get your mind wrapped around it more quickly because I'm dying here." She squirmed beneath him, tightening her legs around him.

He huffed and kissed her, rocking his pelvis against hers in a way that made her whimper. Then they didn't have space for talking because the kiss was too deep, too good.

As they kissed, Scott busied himself in taking off her clothes, so soon she was completely naked beneath him, and she was finding the layers of clothes he still wore increasingly frustrating.

She clawed at his sweater, trying to get it off until he finally reared up, grabbed it by the back, and yanked it off over his head. He did the same with his T-shirt, and her whole body throbbed at the sight of him above her with bare chest, mussed hair, and hot amber eyes.

"Take your jeans off while you're at it," she said, running her hands down his arms from his broad shoulders to his wrists. "They're stiff and scratchy, and I'm much more interested in what's beneath them."

He chuckled as he stood up to shuck his jeans and then his underwear. His naked body was lean, hard, and gorgeous, and her eyes lingered on his full erection, bouncing slightly from his motion.

"Shit," he said before he got back on the bed. "We need a condom."

"I've got some." She reached into the drawer of her

nightstand to find the box, pulling out a packet and handing it to him.

He frowned. "You invite a lot of guys up to this room to use those condoms?"

"You're really getting all macho possessive about that? The two former boyfriends who occasionally spent the night here? You of the fifty-six women?"

His face sobered in a different way as he climbed back onto the bed beside her. "Does it bother you? That there were so many?"

She sighed. "No. Not really. Everyone has a different history."

He reached out to cup her cheek with one hand. "Listen to me, Olivia. I'm not going to say they were meaningless. That would imply they were disposable, and they weren't. They were all other human beings who were giving me something of themselves, and I appreciated and enjoyed them and tried to offer them something back. But I was never fully myself with them. I didn't give any of them all of me. I didn't even understand what it meant to give all of me... until you."

Her eyes blurred over, and her throat tightened.

"Do you believe me?" he asked.

She nodded, swallowing over the emotion. "I believe you. I feel the same way."

"You do?"

"Yes. I do."

His face broke briefly with emotion as he leaned forward to kiss her. She responded, and it deepened fast until they were wrapped up in each other again and rocking together in the rhythm of lovemaking.

Finally Scott pulled away enough to roll on the condom, and then he positioned himself between her legs and teased her entrance until she was gasping.

Then he finally slid himself home.

She moaned at the tightness of the penetration and lifted her legs to twine them around him again, causing him to sink deeper inside her.

"Oh fuck, Olivia." His breath wafted over her skin, adding another layer of sensation. "This is everything. You are.... everything."

She rolled her hips, adjusting to the size of him inside her and processing the honesty of what he'd just said. "I feel that way too."

He eased his hips back and thrust forward, making her arch and gasp. "You like that?"

"Yes." She dug her fingernails into his shoulders.

He thrust again, more forcefully this time. "You need that?"

"Yes! I need more."

"Then I'll give you more. I'll give you everything."

He kissed her again and kept kissing her as they began to rock together, starting slow and steady until hot urgency took over. Eventually they had to break the kiss because their motion was so rough and eager. The bed squeaked shamelessly, and their bodies slapped together, and the sensations coalesced into a hot, intense blur of pleasure.

When she felt an orgasm starting to crest, she strained

toward it, shaking and panting and clawing at his back. She was making a lot of embarrassing sobbing sounds, but she didn't even care.

Scott must have been able to feel how close she was because he pushed into her faster, harder. "Come, Olivia. Come now."

"I'm... trying."

"Oh fuck. Oh please. Come now."

Something about his helpless words and the frantic motion of his body pushed her over the edge. She cried out as release shuddered through her, and she was starting to come down as she realized that Scott had fallen over the edge too.

His thrusting had become rough and jerky, and he was letting out loud grunts with each push. Then an intense pleasure and relief twisted on his face as he let himself go.

She held him as he rode out the spasms, and then she kept holding him as he collapsed on top of her.

She was hot, sweaty, and breathless. She was sore between her legs from two rounds of vigorous sex in one day, and Scott's weight was resting on her fully—heavy and sweltering.

But she wanted it more than anything.

It answered a vacancy in her heart she hadn't even known was there.

She stroked the scratches she'd made in his skin and let her body relax.

"Olivia," he rasped.

It didn't sound like the beginning of a sentence. It sounded like the end.

She smiled.

Maybe in time she'd need some other words, but for now this was more than enough.

12

SCOTT KNEW HE NEEDED TO MOVE, TAKE SOME OF HIS weight off Olivia. He was too heavy to do this to her, and the condom was going to start leaking soon.

But it took a massive effort to make himself roll off her and then another massive effort to sit up on the side of the bed.

He felt almost as shaky as he had this morning when he'd had sex with Olivia for the first time. He hefted himself up, limped to the bathroom attached to her room, and threw the condom away before he washed up. He splashed water on his face and stared at himself in the mirror.

He recognized the unshaven, brown-eyed man in his reflection—with messy hair and a faint scar slashing through his eyebrow from a fall when he was three. But he didn't recognize the look in his eyes. So completely vulnerable. It thrilled and terrified him both.

If Olivia wanted to break him, she could.

"Scott?" She stood in the doorway of the bathroom. She'd pulled her pajamas back on, and she was watching him with a tender wariness that sliced through his heart.

He wasn't going to push her away again, no matter how new this was for him. He walked over and pulled her into a soft hug.

She wrapped her arms around him and burrowed close, emotion shuddering through her body for a few seconds. He leaned down to kiss her when she looked up at him.

"Do you want to come back to bed with me for a while?" she asked.

"Yeah. Yeah, I do."

They returned to bed, and Scott put on his underwear before climbing under the covers beside her. He settled her in his arms so she was pressed up against him.

He was already hot from sex, and her body was very warm, but he didn't care if she made him even hotter. He wasn't going to let her go.

"Scott?" Olivia said after a few minutes.

"Yes." He brushed a kiss into her hair.

"So are we... dating now?"

He released a soft huff of ironic laughter. "Yeah. I guess you could say that."

"Exclusively?"

He tilted his head so he could see her expression. Her eyes were huge and sincere. "Yes. I hope we are."

Her face relaxed, and her inner shining replaced the question in her eyes. “Okay. That sounds good to me.”

“Good. Because I don’t want to be with anyone but you, and I don’t want you to be with anyone but me.”

“That’s what I want too.”

He exhaled deeply and stroked her soft hair. “Thank God. If you told me you wanted to date someone else at the same time, I’m not sure I would have taken it well.”

She giggled. “I wonder what everyone else will say when they find out about us.”

Scott cringed at the thought of telling Kent, who still grumbled every time the Holiday name was mentioned. Kent had borne the brunt of their father’s failures, before and after the feud with Jed Holiday. Phil would probably be happy for him, and Russ...

“Russ was giving me a lecture earlier about stepping up with you, so I think he must already know.”

“Really? I didn’t think anyone knew there was something going on between us. I didn’t even know.”

“I know you didn’t. I knew I’d always been crazy about you, but you never liked me even a little bit.”

“I liked you when we were kids. Once I even tried to learn about model cars so I’d have something to talk about with you.”

Scott stiffened in surprise. “You did?”

“Yes. I was—I don’t know—eleven or twelve. I tried to study up on them and then went to the garage where you were working to talk to you about them.”

He lifted his head, his eyes widening. "That's why you came into the garage that day?"

"Yes. I thought you only saw me as a silly airhead, so I was trying to prove I wasn't, but I got all mixed up and didn't remember what I'd studied, and so I just giggled nervously."

"I thought you were laughing at me!" His brain was nearly exploding at trying to process this new interpretation to an incident that had always needled at him.

"Of course I wasn't laughing at you. Why would I laugh at you? I was the one who couldn't remember any of the names of the cars I'd just memorized, and you were sitting there not saying a word like you thought I was an idiot. So I just giggled and made up an excuse and ran away as fast as I could." She exhaled deeply as she stroked his chest, playing with the light scattering of dark hair there. "I wasn't used to people not liking me, and I didn't know why you didn't, so I just assumed you thought I was stupid."

"I never thought you were stupid. I've always been tongue-tied around you."

"I didn't know that. It never even occurred to me. So when you changed and started going out with all those scads of women but never even looked at me twice, I just assumed you still didn't like me. It bothered me. I didn't understand it. And you were so mean after we found out... found out about Dad."

"I know I was. I'm so sorry for that. I was hurt and angry, but that's no excuse. I think it was worse with you because it felt like I'd lost you forever—even though I'd never had you. I'm so sorry for acting that way."

"I forgive you. I wasn't very nice to you either, even later when things should have gotten better between us. I still had to hold on to this idea that I didn't like you because otherwise... Maybe that was why you were always able to rile me up. I didn't realize it was because I wanted more from you."

"I'm glad we figured it out."

"Me too. Laura isn't going to like it. She already thinks things have gotten too sappy with Phil and Rebecca, so another couple is going to push her over the edge. It's kind of funny that it's two Holiday-Matheson couples."

"I don't know." He was feeling completely relaxed now. Sated and happy and drowsy and tender. "Our families have always been tangled up together. We've always been part of each other's lives. I think it kind of fits."

"Yeah. Maybe it does."

They drifted into silence, and then Olivia drifted into sleep.

It wasn't long until Scott drifted off too.

They dozed for less than an hour before Olivia woke him by climbing out of the bed.

"Sorry," she said when he opened his eyes. "I need to pee."

He chuckled and watched her pad barefoot across the room, and he stretched out when she closed the door.

They hadn't had any lunch, and he was getting hungry. He wouldn't say no to some food.

Reaching down for his clothes on the floor, he pulled them on so he was fully dressed when Olivia came back into the room.

"Where are you going?" she asked, her lips turning down as she looked at him from head to toe.

"Sorry. I just realized I'm starving. I've got to get something to eat."

"Oh." A little smile twitched on the corners of her mouth. "Now that you mention it, I'm kind of hungry too. We can go down to the shop and get a sandwich or something if you want. Just let me throw on some clothes."

"Perfect."

She put on jeans and a red top before sliding on a pair of shoes. He took her hand as they left the room, and he was still holding it when they ran into Laura in the living room.

She took in their rumpled appearance and their clasped hands and then scowled at them. "What the hell? You're supposed to not like each other."

"We do," Olivia said, her cheeks flushing.

Laura rolled her eyes. "Is it something in the water? Or is it just that it's a week until Christmas and everyone is embracing maudlin sentimentality? Why is everyone suddenly trying to pair off? Even people who should really know better."

Her questions were more vehement than the situation called for, so something else must have set her off.

"Who else is pairing off?" Olivia asked.

Laura's expression was momentarily trapped, and it told Scott something.

He suddenly remembered what Russ had told him about stepping up with the woman he loved and it not working.

Had something happened between Russ and Laura? Something that was upsetting her now?

"No one," Laura said, her expression clearing with her typical control. "It's just that Penny got back a few minutes ago. Her car is still in a ditch, so Kent had to drive her. And —I don't know—they're acting weird." She made a frustrated sound, glancing back down at where Scott was still holding Olivia's hand in his. "So you guys are a done deal then?"

Scott met Olivia's eyes when she glanced over at him. He smiled. "Yeah. We're a done deal."

Laura made a face. "Just perfect. Now other people are going to get more ideas."

She didn't explain what she meant by that, but Scott was pretty sure he already knew.

A week later, Scott woke up on Christmas morning in Olivia's bed.

She was still sleeping on her side, her loose hair

spilling all around her face and shoulders and her arms curled up toward her chest. Her lashes were thick and her breathing was steady, and the bare skin of her neck and shoulders made him want to do things.

All kinds of things.

He'd been with her for a week now, and they'd had sex every day, but it wasn't even close to enough.

That night they'd shared in the cottage, he'd believed his heart couldn't contain any more feeling. But he'd been wrong. The pressure he felt in his chest as he gazed at her sleeping right now was even stronger, even bigger than it had been last week.

If it kept up like this, there would be no way his chest could contain all that he felt for her.

As he watched, her lashes started to flutter, and then she opened her eyes.

She smiled sleepily, her warm spirit shining out in her eyes, her mouth, her whole self. "Hi."

"Hi."

"Merry Christmas."

"Merry Christmas to you too." He brushed her hair back behind her ear, letting his fingertips linger on her cheek.

"You're looking kind of sappy this morning," she said.

"Am I?"

"Yeah. But I don't mind. Christmas is a good time for sappiness. And you haven't had nearly enough sappiness in your life, so you have a lot of time to make up for."

He chuckled and reached over to take her hand, stroking her palm with his thumb.

"Are you ready for all the chaos today?" she asked in a different tone. "I've got to warn you, it gets crazy around here on Christmas."

"I've already gotten a taste of the craziness over the past few days. And if it means I get to spend Christmas with you, then I'm not about to complain."

Her smile beamed for a moment. "Who knew Scott Matheson could be so sweet?"

"Only you. Only you get to know."

"Let's keep it that way, okay?"

He cleared his throat. He hadn't intended to say anything. They'd only been together for a week. But she was looking at him like… And he was so full of feeling he couldn't wait any longer. "I'm good with keeping it that way forever."

Her breath hitched as she processed what he said.

His heart hammered when she didn't reply immediately.

Shit.

Maybe he'd moved too fast. Maybe she wasn't ready. Maybe he'd blown the best thing that had ever happened to him.

"Do you mean that?" she asked at last.

"Yeah. Yeah, I do. I know it's soon. It's too soon. But I'm falling in love with you, and I can't help it." He blurted the words out, knowing they were a risk, knowing he was showing her everything.

She made a little whimper of sound, her face tightening. She reached out to stroke his face. "I know it's soon, but it doesn't seem to matter. We've been tangled up together all our lives, and I've known you forever. I'm falling in love with you too. Maybe I have been for a long time. But I know it now, and I don't think it's going to go away."

He let out an embarrassingly helpless sound as he pulled her into his arms.

He hadn't blown it after all.

He'd maybe even done something right.

"This is it for me," he murmured. "There's not going to be anyone else for me."

"Me either." She pulled back so she could smile at him. "You're number six for me, and I'm number fifty-seven for you, and the count stops there for good."

He laughed and pulled her into a tight hug. "It's a deal. Although, to tell you the truth, you were always number one for me. I just never thought a miracle would happen and I'd actually get to have you."

"Christmas is the time for miracles. You do have me. So what are you going to do with me?"

It wasn't even seven yet on Christmas morning. They had plenty of time before breakfast.

So Scott showed her exactly what he was going to do with her.

He was planning to keep showing her for the rest of their lives.

EPILOGUE

ONE YEAR LATER

Olivia was hot, sweaty, and irritable, and Scott was making it worse.

What was supposed to be a pleasant two-hour hike in the woods had turned into a three-and-a-half-hour exercise in frustration, and she was in a bad mood by the time she finally reached the Mistletoe Cottage and keyed in the code to open the door.

It was blessedly cool inside. At least that was something.

Scott stepped inside right behind her, and she could feel heat and tension coming off him, although he hadn't said anything for a full five minutes.

He was in a bad mood too.

She should be a grown-up. Take a shower and retire to separate quarters for a while until both of them had cooled down.

They'd been together for a year now. She had experience in being in a relationship with him. She knew how to avoid making an argument worse.

She wiped the sweat off her cheeks and forehead with the sleeve of the long-sleeve T-shirt she'd been stupid enough to wear.

"Are you going to stand there stewing all day?" Scott demanded.

Snapping at him will just make it worse.

Don't make it worse. Don't make it worse. Don't make it worse.

"I'll stand here stewing for as long as I want!"

Scott was even sweatier than she was, and his brown eyes were fixed in a glare on her face. "Fine. Then I'll go take a shower."

She sucked in a sharp breath. "Why do you get to take a shower first?"

"Because you're standing there stewing."

"I'm perfectly capable of stewing in the shower, you know. You think my stewing abilities are geographically limited?"

"I think your stewing abilities are second to none."

"You've barely scratched the surface of my stewing abilities."

They glared at each other for several seconds, and Olivia hoped Scott was struggling for a good retort, which meant her last verbal thrust had been a success.

But then she saw Scott's lips twitch just slightly.

She stiffened. "Don't you dare, Scott."

The corner of his mouth twitched again, so briefly it was barely perceptible.

"I have legitimate grievances here. You don't get to make me laugh and get out of the fight prematurely."

His whole face twisted for a moment in what she knew was an attempt to control his amusement. Then his features settled into a look of exaggerated sobriety. "I'm not laughing. Go ahead and let me have it."

She stared at him for a long moment, torn between annoyance, amusement, and affection. Then she gave up and made a loud, impatient sound as she turned on her heel. "Damn it, Scott." Her tone wasn't really angry anymore. "You're the most frustrating man in the world. You know that, right?"

"So I've been told." There was a teasing lilt in his voice now. "Usually by you."

When she stepped into the bathroom, she closed the door with a loud click. Then she opened it again and said through the crack, "You can share the shower with me if you want."

She'd peeled off her clothes and stepped under the warm spray when Scott joined her.

The bathroom boasted what they advertised as a couple's shower, so there were two rainfall showerheads and they didn't have to both try to use one. Olivia soaped up and rinsed off, occasionally checking out Scott, who was washing the sweat off his naked body with a no-nonsense efficiency she couldn't help but find a bit sexy.

When he'd cleaned himself up, he stepped over under her spray.

"Hey," she objected without any heat. "This is my side."

"If you didn't want me on your side, then you shouldn't be standing there naked. What's a man supposed to do when the most beautiful woman in the world is right there, naked in the shower?"

Despite his words, he didn't make a move on her. Instead, he pulled her into his arms.

She'd cooled off and no longer felt hot and gross, so the embrace was nice.

Nice and unexpectedly tender.

She leaned her cheek against his shoulder. "I'm not the most beautiful woman in the world."

He nuzzled the side of her head. "We've already had this discussion many times, and we'll have to agree to disagree on this matter."

Her arms were twined around his neck, and she played with his wet hair with one hand. "I was right about which trail we should have taken."

"Yes, you were. But in my defense, there was no way either one of us could have known about that mudslide."

She sighed and relaxed against him even more. He was starting to get aroused. She could feel his erection nudging. But there was nothing particularly urgent about his body yet, and she felt more emotional than sexy at the moment. "I know that. But still. If we'd gone the other way like I wanted, we wouldn't have had to backtrack and walk in this heat for an extra hour."

"That is true."

"Why the hell is it so hot in December?" she burst out, reminded of her primary source of grievance. "It's a week before Christmas, and we were supposed to have a cozy, romantic weekend."

"It can still be a cozy, romantic weekend." He was nuzzling her again.

"If we turn the air conditioner down enough, maybe we can even make a fire." She scowled against his shoulder. "This time last year we had snow."

"Do you really want a snowstorm like that again?"

"I don't know. Being stranded in the snow with you again doesn't sound like the worst idea in the world. Look what happened last year."

Scott pulled back and met her eyes. "I know what happened last year. You think I'm ever going to forget it?"

"No. Not really. Since you're stuck with me now." She smiled as she lifted her left hand and looked down at the rings she wore. The diamond engagement ring he'd given her five months ago and the wedding ring he'd put on her finger two weeks ago. "You're stuck with me forever."

"Sounds about right to me." He kissed her then, and it was slow and deep and lovely.

Her husband was kissing her.

Scott was her husband.

The idea of it was still new, delightful, thrilling.

She still felt like giggling every time she realized it was true.

She assumed that would wear off eventually, but she didn't think it would happen soon.

When Scott finally pulled out of the kiss, she reached over and turned off the water in the shower, and he moved over to turn off the spray on the other side. They dried off and put on the white bathrobes hanging on the hooks. Instead of trying to dry her hair, she pulled it into two braids.

She felt clean and tired and relaxed as they left the bathroom. "Do you want something to drink?" she asked.

"Yeah. But I guess it better be water after the heat and the hiking."

She grabbed two bottles of sparkling water from the wine cooler and carried them over to the couch. Scott was fiddling with the air conditioner.

"Did you turn it cooler?" she asked when he came to join her.

"Yeah." His mouth turned up in a wry smile. "We can make a fire later."

She giggled and cuddled up against him. But she sighed again as she looked at the empty fireplace. "Why does it have to be so hot?"

"Because it's Virginia, and Virginia likes to mess you around just for fun."

She laughed again before she adjusted so she could see his face. "Did you want to have sex?"

He was halfway through a swig of his water, but he pulled the bottle away from his mouth with a popping sound. "What do you think?"

She felt inside his robe until she could wrap a hand around his erection. "I think you might want to have sex."

His smile was hot and tender. "But if you're too tired or not in the mood, I really don't mind."

"I'm not too tired, as long as you do most of the work."

"That sounds perfectly acceptable to me." He put both their water bottles onto the side table and then rolled them over so she was on her back and he was above her, his lower body between her legs. "How's this?"

"This is good. But I think we better put a blanket beneath us. This is a good couch, and poor Harriet would have to try to clean it if things got messy."

He made a choked burst of laughter and groaned as he stood up, helping her stand up too and then spreading a throw blanket out on the couch. "Okay?"

"Yes. Okay." She slanted him a quick glance. "You still in the mood?"

"You think a few logistical maneuvers is going to stop me from being in the mood? I've wanted you most of my life, and now you're my wife. I could make love to you until the end of the world, and it still wouldn't be enough."

Washed with pleasure and deep affection, she lay back down on the couch and pulled him on top of her. "I'm not sure we're up to apocalyptic sex this afternoon, but we'll do the best we can."

"You have no idea how apocalyptic I can be."

"Then I guess you better show me."

So he did.

ABOUT NOELLE ADAMS

Noelle handwrote her first romance novel in a spiral-bound notebook when she was twelve, and she hasn't stopped writing since. She has lived in eight different states and currently resides in Virginia, where she writes full time, reads any book she can get her hands on, and offers tribute to a very spoiled cocker spaniel.

She loves travel, art, history, and ice cream. After spending far too many years of her life in graduate school, she has decided to reorient her priorities and focus on writing contemporary romances. For more information, please check out her website: noelle-adams.com.

Made in the USA
Middletown, DE
30 April 2025